Who knew what accounted for it? Maybe her thick
cascade of curly chestnut hair. She had imagined how,
pulled back with one hand, it would be full, soft and
springy in her palm, and how it would expose her
throat, a sloping, swan's neck throat, pale and a little
over-delicate with age. She had imagined her breasts
and large, dark nipples. She had imagined as far as the
musky smell of her, the sticky, welcoming taste of
her . . .

DIANE SALVATORE

PAXTON COURT

DIANE SALVATORE

PAXTON COURT

NAIAD
1995

Printed in the United States of America on acid-free paper
First Hard Back Edition 1995
First Trade Paper Back Edition 1996

Editor: Christine Cassidy
Cover designer: Catherine Hopkins
Typesetter: Sandi Stancil

Library of Congress Cataloging-in-Publication Data

Salvatore, Diane.
    Paxton Court / by Diane Salvatore.
        p.   cm.
    ISBN 1-56280-114-7
    I. Title.
PS3569.A46234P39   1995
813'.54—dc20   95-14533
                                                                    CIP

ABOUT THE AUTHOR

Diane Salvatore's first novel, *Benediction,* was a finalist for a Lambda Literary Award in 1991. She is also the author of *Love, Zena Beth* and *Not Telling Mother: Stories From A Life.* She is deputy editor at a national woman's magazine, and lives in New Jersey with her partner of 13 years and their cocker spaniel.

1

*F*elicia Olson was proud to consider herself the unofficial, one-woman welcoming committee of Lakeside Leisure, the preeminent retirement community of southwestern Florida. Or at least she thought it so, with the chauvinism that was as inevitable in these matters as palmetto bugs at a pool party.

So far, May had been a very busy month. Four new houses, all built in the last year, were occupied nearly all at once, and attractive, unusual houses they were, too. Builders from New York City, she had learned, had been brought in, and the results were . . . well, conspicuous. She knew some Lakesiders were upset, calling the houses showy and other less flattering things she did not think kind to repeat, even to herself. Secretly, she liked the vividness of the houses — secretly because there was no reason to announce your disagreement if it wouldn't change anything and would just upset people further. At thirty-five hundred square feet, the new houses were easily bigger by a third than the biggest houses currently in Lakeside, and she knew that alone steamed some residents, especially people like Bunny and Bill Seagirt, who had a very Cro-Magnon attitude about it, and were satisfied only when their campfire was the biggest and brightest around.

But it wasn't just the size. It was the colors. The new houses, which took up all of Paxton Court, were bold and arresting shades of lavender with plum, mauve with maroon, and other colors she'd not yet been able to pin down by name. Extras they all knew could mean the difference between paying for your daughters' weddings or not — Spanish tile roofs, field-stone facades, lavish landscaping, stained glass, marble-accented entranceways — were also in evidence. This was met with admiration and envy, Felicia knew, a combustible combination that did not always win friends.

Felicia and her husband, Ted, had been Lakesiders longer than any of their friends. At sixty-eight, they were a good five years older than the others. They had bought when the community was brand new, just a huge expanse of land, a few model homes, and someone's imagination about how it would one day feel like a little resort. The prices of the houses had been much more modest then, the better to attract initial buyers. With each passing year, as it grew more popular and solvent, she and Ted watched as the new houses dwarfed their own in size and ambition. That was just fine with them, since they calculated their own property's worth as increasing with their neighbors'.

And that meant more money to leave to their kids, of course.

Felicia had made her visit to three of the houses earlier this month. At the first, a very sweet-looking lady had answered the door — younger, frankly, than Felicia had expected, but then, people today seemed eager to retire earlier and earlier. (Ted insisted it had nothing to do with free will, only that the poor economy was pushing people over fifty-five out of their jobs, but Felicia hadn't been able to confirm this yet because it was a very tacky thing to ask a person.) Felicia had held out her offering of cups of sugar, salt and flour, and explained the usual about it being for luck and happiness in a new home. The woman had seemed a little jumpy, wiping her palms on her jeans and eyeing Felicia warily, as if Felicia were leftovers she thought maybe had turned. The woman introduced herself as Karen, said thanks and seemed relieved to be shutting the door.

At the second house, a wonderful aroma had come wafting out as a terrific-looking man, all jawline and cleft chin and thick silver hair, opened the door. Felicia introduced herself and commented on what a marvelous cook his wife must be. "Not my wife," Rich, as he instructed Felicia to call him, had corrected. She had been immediately embarrassed, felt her earlobes and her cheeks burn with it. But the man had smiled impishly, as if he had made a good joke, and promised he'd invite her and Ted over one night to sample the cooking. As she headed back down the driveway, she reprimanded herself about not being so conventional. These fifty and sixty year olds today — they didn't always retire with a legal spouse.

At the third house, a tall, elegant woman —

3

handsome was the word people would use — had come to the door. Felicia was reminded that she had heard from someone that one of the new buyers was a doctor. "Are you the doctor's wife?" Felicia had asked after handing over her good-luck cups. The woman had smiled slowly and answered, "Actually, we're both doctors."

Now Felicia was at the door of the last house, the lavender one. Again a woman answered, this one petite and brown-haired and carrying stained gardener's gloves. A glossy springer spaniel eased out impatiently alongside her leg, nostrils flexing in the breeze.

"Good morning," Felicia said, holding her cups out in front of her and delivering her welcome comments. Something about the woman's green eyes and keen, interested expression made Felicia feel especially sincere about the good wishes.

"Well, how completely unexpected and *nice,*" the woman said. "I'm Helen. This is Emma," she said, trailing her fingertips along the dog's head. "Come in and have some coffee."

Felicia tried her best to decline — she didn't like to look as though she were nosing around — but the woman nearly dragged her in by the elbow, surprising Felicia with her strength.

The house was grand — breathtaking even — by Felicia's standards, but Helen seemed to have no inclination to show it off, which only made Felicia like her more. Still, while Helen fixed the coffee in the kitchen, and Emma lay on the rug, Felicia settled on the teal leather couch and tried to memorize the details so she could go back and relay it all to Ted. The living room and dining room were done in teal and bronze, and both rooms shared a panoramic view of the enclosed outdoor pool. Sculptures, many of them female nudes, Felicia noted with a blush, sat atop the glass and lacquer tables or in corners of the rooms on their own stands. Sleek club chairs, black with a splash of bronze, accented the living room, while a frosted glass orb chandelier, something like a spaceship, presided over the dining room.

"How's that?" Helen asked, coming in from the kitchen and handing Felicia a mug with a bold, swirling oriental design. Felicia noticed all these little details, because she liked little details. It was these details that she'd been too busy her whole life — teaching and cooking and cleaning and raising two kids — to dwell on, and now she was happy to be able to. Felicia sipped the coffee gratefully — it had an unusual, hazelnut flavor — as Helen sat in one of club chairs, which, to Felicia's amazement, rocked. The spaniel got up and moved closer to Helen's feet.

"So, have you met all your new neighbors yet?" Felicia asked. "It worked out so nicely that you all moved into the court at the same time."

"*Those* neighbors? We're old friends. Practically family," Helen said. We arranged to retire together. It's all completely by design."

"No! That's too perfect. I had no idea. How do you all know each other? Were you all neighbors somewhere else?"

"Oh, no, no," Helen said. "But close enough, as the northeast goes. Manhattan. North Jersey. Long Island. Brooklyn Heights."

"And children?"

"Not all of us."

Felicia took this to mean Helen did not have any, and she felt sad, because Helen had a natural warmth well suited to motherhood.

"I'm a professional dog handler. I traveled for most of my career."

"How *interesting,*" Felicia said. "I've never in all my life met a dog handler. But I just have the feeling you were probably one of the best around."

Helen smiled, and appealing wrinkles, the only ones she seemed to have, fanned out delicately from the corners of her eyes. "I enjoyed it. And I'll miss it." She looked out across the room absentmindedly, letting her hand roam over the dog's neck. "I'm not used to being retired yet but my partner and I made all the money we want and we decided to take some time to enjoy ourselves before, you know, all we're doing is testing our blood sugar and oiling the wheelchair." Helen laughed.

"Yes, that's smart," Felicia said, seizing on and storing away the word *partner* for future examination. She scanned Helen's hands and registered only a striking gold and coral ring that didn't look to her like a wedding band. So far, that meant two out of four of the new couples weren't married. Maybe she had lost track, maybe marriage had fallen out of favor up in the Hudson valley. "Well, listen, maybe Ted and I can take you two out to dinner one night soon," Felicia said, getting up, not wanting to make a pest of herself.

"We'd like that," Helen said, walking her to the door, with Emma shadowing them.

When Felicia was back out on the sidewalk, blinking in the sunshine, she cursed herself for forgetting to get even the "partner's" name.

2

*H*elen had called the whole gang the second Felicia Olson was out of view, but only Rudy and Rich were around, and it took them nearly a half hour to amble over from just a few hundred yards away. Rich, no doubt fresh from a swim, had his silver hair slicked back. Long-limbed and angular in his black tank top and perfectly creased khaki shorts, he added his usual jolt of elegance to the room. Rudy, compact, olive-skinned, and bald (first for fashion, later for function) lounged on the floor, flopping Emma's ears over her eyes as she wagged her backside in joyful submission. Rich dropped to the floor across from him, and Helen watched, with parental pride, as they made Emma play doggie-in-the-middle with a caterpillar squeak toy. Her tongue lolled crazily as she ran from one of her laughing uncles to the other. Helen slipped out to drag Lara in from poolside, where she'd fallen asleep, a Stephen Hawking hardcover resting on her stomach. Lara came in, rubbing her eyes, and kissed first Rich, then Rudy, on the tops of their heads.

"What's so important that you had to wake me from dreams of quarks and black holes?" Lara asked, falling heavily into one of the club chairs and stretching hard.

"Lara, I asked you not to talk about your sex life in mixed company," Rudy teased.

Helen saw she was going to have trouble getting them all to be serious this morning. "Look, I want to know what we're saying to everyone, since these are going to be our neighbors until eternity."

"Helen, you're such a worrier," Rich said. "We've talked about this for years, since we first started looking for a place to retire. You know what my attitude is," he said, jerking forward in a tug-of-war he was losing to Emma over the caterpillar.

"Remind me — I'm old now, remember?" Helen said.

"Just go about my business. Exactly what I did when Felicia came to our door. I'll invite her and her husband to dinner one night and there Rudy and I'll both be. We don't have to hang a banner saying we sleep together for it to be obvious."

"Think again," Rudy said. "Down here, when they say 'sleep together,' there's a good chance they mean it literally."

"Rudy's got a point," Lara said, slouching deeply in her chair and unbuttoning a top button on her Izod. "We can't assume this crowd'll catch on to all the cues. But that's fine by me. Ambiguity is a very good neighbor."

Just then, the caterpillar, breaking free of Emma's clenched jaw and Rich's grip, sailed through the air and bounced hard off Lara's temple in a spray of spittle.

"Goddamn it, Rich! Watch what you're doing, will ya?"

At the sound of Lara's raised voice, Emma rushed to Helen's legs, and sat as politely as an altar girl.

"Oooh, someone woke up on the wrong side of the lounge chair," Rich said.

"Yeah, yeah," Lara said, smoothing her short, ash-brown hair. She had only recently begun dyeing it, after it had gone completely gray, and Helen knew she still felt self-conscious about her concession to vanity.

"All right, so we agree we won't torture anyone?" Helen said. "She seemed like a sweet old lady."

"Hey, don't talk torture to us," said Rudy who, in a red and turquoise Hawaiian shirt and black nylon running shorts, so far seemed to think he was only on extended vacation. "It's Angie and Ruth you'll have to declaw."

"True," Helen said. Ruth and Angie almost hadn't agreed to move down with them, vowing to wait until there was an exclusively gay and lesbian retirement village. Helen took it personally, since she had done the bulk of the research for their retirement spot, cross-referencing taxes with temperatures with proximity to major airports. And Lakeside Leisure's setting was both gorgeous and affordable enough that Helen had begun to push hard for it. Besides, she and Lara didn't like the idea of separatism; they believed it was important to live openly among straights, and not go creating closets, even if they were as big as stadiums.

And they might all be dead, Helen argued, before they found something ideal in all ways. Ruth and Angie had reluctantly agreed, with the warning that they planned to be as out as ever and not care whose pacemaker they taxed.

"Did they hang out their pink triangle flag yet?" Rudy asked, coaxing Emma back over by gyrating the squeak toy.

"No, but I think I saw their mailbox painted 'Stars and Dykes Forever,' " Rich said, giggling.

"Don't even *joke* like that in front of them," Lara said. "You'll give them ideas."

"So, is this meeting of Lesbian Lakesiders adjourned?" Rudy asked, getting up. "We're going to take a drive up north, see how far we are from gay civilization." Helen knew by that he meant a gay bar.

"Thanks, guys. I'll walk you out," Helen said, leashing Emma and taking her along. The air was rapidly losing its early morning coolness and taking on the steamy heat of afternoon.

"I don't know what to blame Lara's snits on anymore," Rich said, "ever since she's stopped being premenstrual for good."

"Don't be so hard on her," Helen said. "I think she's having status deprivation. It's hard to go from being a partner at a Wall Street law firm to being head weed-picker."

"I thought she was going to write that book, the one about queer discrimination?" Rich asked. "It'd be great. She should do it."

Helen took his arm and leaned into him happily. It was one of the things she loved about Rich, his always believing that people were capable of great things, that solutions were always just around the corner. She associated that attitude, free as it was of the complications of personality and mood swings, with masculinity, and it amused her to imagine occasionally, through him, what it might have been like to live with a man. "I've been telling her the same thing," Helen said, "but I don't think she's figured out yet how to function down here. I don't think she knows how to work unless she's got eighteen-hour heartburn."

"That's the phone," Rudy said, as they got to the door. He rushed inside, leaving Helen alone with Rich.

"And how are you two adjusting?" she asked.

"Good, I think. Rudy's still debating doing the catering business. I think he's afraid of us having too much time together, just in case, after twenty years, we discover we don't really like each other."

Helen smiled. As a bank vice president, Rich had had day hours, and as a chef, Rudy had worked a lot of nights. A schedule like that would have broken up most women, Helen and Lara had always agreed, but it seemed to have worked for Rudy and Rich.

"Well, have fun scoping out gay life forms," she said, reaching up to take his cheeks in her hands and give him a loud kiss on the lips. Emma stamped her feet and whimpered.

"Women," Rich said smiling, giving the springer a quick scratch behind the ear. "Such a jealous bunch."

3

*B*unny Seagirt watched the kiss on Paxton Court through the telescope in her living room, two blocks away. Bill bought it recently to look at stars, a big waste of time, Bunny was quick to tell him, but she didn't mind having spent the money since, she had discovered, the telescope's uses during the day were myriad and meaningful.

So this is what they could expect from their colorful new neighbors: Illicit affairs with each other's husbands in broad daylight right under each other's front awnings. Unless, of course, it wasn't technically an affair, but something worse, something like wife swapping or swinging or whatever it was called that she had seen on *Oprah*. It would be just like Felicia to have missed the clues and nuances. What was it Felicia had said the woman told her? They were like *family*, that was it. Well, she was probably winking when she said it. She probably meant commune, and of course it went right over Felicia's head. She had recognized the man from Felicia's description — the good looking one, wasn't it always the way? And the woman, since she had the dog with her, had to be Helen, who Felicia was so fond of already. Well, Bunny would see how fond Felicia was when she found out that Helen was schtupping the man next door, and so hot and heavy about it that she couldn't resist a big wet kiss not a hundred yards from her own front door.

"Felicia, it's Bunny," she said into the phone, barely letting Felicia finish saying hello. She described what she had just seen and speculated. "And you had to see them — *cleaving* to each other like dogs in heat."

"Bunny, you spy on people through a *telescope?*"

"It was just like Felicia to completely miss the point. "Did you hear what I just told you? They're either a bunch of flagrant adulterers, or they're running some kind of sex ring over there. It's an outrage!"

"Oh, I don't know, Bunny. I think you've been watching too many of those cable movies on the Playboy channel. Nothing that interesting happens down here."

"It's Bill, I'm very sorry to say, who watches the Playboy channel. And I wouldn't call this *interesting*, Felicia. I'd call it *immoral.*"

"Who was the second man?"

"I assume it was Helen's husband. And as soon as

the poor man had his back turned, his wife had her fingers all tangled up in her sweetie's hair, and was giving him this big, open-mouthed smooch."

"That must be an awfully impressive telescope, Bunny. Has Bill spotted life on Jupiter yet?"

"Don't sass me, Felicia. You'll see. I told you anyone who builds a purple house can't be up to any good!"

4

*L*ara was waiting for Helen when she came back, and she offered to take Emma for a walk. She felt guilty for having yelled at the poor dog for simply having a good time with her uncles.

She strolled with Emma toward Chris and Karen's house. Lara had known Chris since their law school days together, and after Helen, Chris was her best friend. The automatic garage door was just lifting for their car as Lara and Emma rounded the corner. Chris, who was driving, honked the horn in greeting. "Hey girl," she said, as Emma bounded over the moment Chris opened the car door.

"Good morning," Lara said. "I just came by to see if I could interest someone in a stroll." Karen, lifting grocery bags out of the hatchback, gave what Lara felt was a distracted smile. She seemed to be absorbing sun every moment; her arms and legs were already the color of light toast. At just fifty, she was the youngest of their group, and she looked it.

"You go ahead, Chris. There's not much to do here," Karen said, bustling toward the side door.

"No, I'll help you put the stuff away," Chris said, but Karen shooed her, and Lara, feeling too selfish to be polite, didn't object.

The two friends and Emma — delighted, evidently, to have increased the size of her pack by one — headed down the wide, sun-bleached sidewalk. Long, curving streets stretched in all directions, and pastel houses with different configurations of palm trees and orange trees were spaced evenly on lush, green lawns.

"You have that Is-this-all-there-is look on your face," Chris said. "You used to look like that when we met for lunch in Manhattan and you were having a slow week between crises."

Lara laughed. "I never could get away with much with you."

"You told me to remind you, when you had days like this, that you were doing this for you and Helen. So you two could finally have some time together, instead of calling each other from airport telephones all the time."

"You're right," Lara said, feeling a wave of nostalgia for those whispered phone calls when they'd lament how much they missed each other. Sometimes they'd be apart for two weeks at a time, and Lara never got used to it, the sleeping alone in hotel beds, without even the comforting smell of Helen's scalp lingering on the pillow next to her. Everything felt foreign and sterile without Helen beside her. "I'm just having a little trouble with all this unscheduled time." Everyone kept urging her to relax, but she was discovering she really didn't enjoy relaxation. "Have you looked into that pro bono work yet?"

"Yes, actually," Chris said. "There's a lot of very important environmental work down here—developers trying to pave over the most amazing plots of land that support endangered plant and animal life. I might start on a case as soon as next week."

"Really? Great."

Chris was an ACLU lawyer her whole career, defending the civil rights of blacks, gays, the homeless and the mentally ill. Lara, with her corporate clients, had made about three times what Chris had and yet Chris had never made her feel guilty or sleazy about the embezzlers, polluters, monopolizers and tax cheats Lara's firm routinely represented. In fact, Lara had ended up envying Chris more than the reverse, she was sure. Especially these days. Lara had made money, but she felt Chris had made a difference.

"You know, maybe you should think of this as changing jobs," Chris said. "You have to give yourself time to adjust. Assume there's potential to enjoy yourself. For one thing, you gotta admit the dress code here is a lot more civilized."

Lara laughed, eyeing them both in their denim shorts and neon sneakers. She recalled now with amazement the level of physical discomfort she had put up with in corporate women's clothes her whole adult life: pantyhose that were never quite long enough to reach her crotch, pumps that nipped her pinkie toes, starched blouses that pulled across her broad shoulders, and, when the fashions turned "mod," skirts that rode up her thighs and had to be wrestled back to

17

propriety. And the constant clothes shopping — lest you ever be caught in last year's styles — and the maintenance by way of dry cleaning and early-morning pressing. She shuddered at the memory. She had been convinced all along it was a plot. The energy she had spent *looking* the part would have been so much better spent acting it. Yes, she admitted, there were very tangible pleasures attached to being retired.

"And how's Karen adjusting?" Lara asked, feeling guilty about focusing on herself so long.

"She's got her studio all set up. She wants to do my portrait."

"Ah, does she do the ones where you stay young forever, or just the regular kind?"

"Lara, none of us has been young in about twenty years."

Chris had just celebrated her sixty-second birthday. She'd gone gray in her forties, but other than that, Lara thought, her old friend was much the same as always — the same square-jawed face and gray-green eyes, the same goofy sense of humor and husky laugh. Lara thought Chris was still attractive, if a little weather-beaten, and she had never understood why Chris hadn't been more in demand, why her love life had always been so full of shrieking battles and bitter disappointments, until, that is, Karen came along. "When we were twenty-one," Lara said, "we used to call people our age elderly."

"I know. Which is why I feel completely justified now calling twenty-one-year-olds nitwits."

5

*B*ill Seagirt had never met a woman he didn't like, but that was because he made a point of not meeting the ones who didn't comply with his criteria. Fortunately, this was easy to accomplish, since his criteria could be spotted at fifty paces.

So when he spied the buxom number in the mint-green short set peevishly palming the broccoli, he pushed his shopping cart eagerly in her direction. As he got closer, he smiled to himself. She had the three B's: brunette, brown-eyed and bosomy. The only one of those his wife really had left was the brown eyes.

"You know your vegetables. I can tell from the way you're sizing up that broccoli," he said, adopting the tone of concerned consumer and noting that she wore only a pinkie ring, no wedding band. "I'm making a salad that calls for Bibb lettuce, and I wouldn't know Bibb from Boston from Romaine if I had a gun to my temple." He smiled confidently; this was invariably where the woman, compelled by the urge to educate and rescue, took him by the wrist and spoke engagingly about the shapes and hues of lettuce leaves while he assessed if she were willing to cheat on her husband, or, when it came to widows, at least his memory.

Instead, this woman looked at him with the mild surprise of someone who didn't expect this particular stranger next to her to possess the necessary mental skills required for speech. "It tells you up top," she said pointing at the brightly colored plastic directionals. "There are even little pictures." Then she turned and wheeled away, her shapely butt wagging off into the distance.

A carbonated mix of anger, humiliation and disbelief bubbled in his gut. He wasn't used to being brushed off, and unkindly, too. He knew he was a good-looking man — for his age, though he hated that expression. Tanned and toned from golfing, with all his hair yet, and what had been called a dapper moustache, women regularly went pink-cheeked when he paid attention to them, even if they hadn't been willing to slip him between their air-conditioned marital sheets.

He decided this one must be a little slow or a little shy. Yes, surely that was it. He smoothed his moustache with his thumb and forefinger and then shoved his empty cart after her.

"I'm Bill," he said when his cart was flush with

hers. Her powdery fragrance reached his nostrils and emboldened him. "I hope you didn't think I was rude back there."

She stopped her cart abruptly and scowled. "Well, I hope you thought *I* was, because I meant to be." Then she pushed forward ferociously, nearly stepping out of her mint green loafers as she strode off.

He couldn't have been more shocked if she'd slapped him. But now he was determined — and intrigued. And the sight of her slender ankles above her loafers convinced him she was worth a little more effort than usual.

He caught up with her just as she was turning her cart sharply right, and he broadsided it with his own. The rattling collision caused a few heads to turn, but fortunately no one saw anything interesting enough to stare — just, he knew, a couple of old people daffy enough to have a cart crash. He watched the color rise up from her neck into her cheeks, like beets bleeding into mashed potatoes.

"Oh — so sorry," he said, smiling, affecting a slightly dangerous look this time. Maybe she didn't go for the sweet and befuddled type. "I think we're destined to keep meeting."

She leaned over their tangled carts, her cleavage revealed prettily. "Keep it up mister," she whispered menacingly, "and the next thing to get rammed is going to be your nuts."

He pulled back, repelled, his dignity completely assaulted. He'd done nothing to deserve such insult. In fact, it was an extremely ungracious way to repay the compliment of his attention. He hadn't felt so degraded since high school when the homecoming queen had laughed in his face when he asked her to dance. Now he didn't care who heard him.

"You old dyke," he said, with the vengeance of the ages.

She glared at him and there it was again, that same brand of mocking, self-congratulatory female laughter he recognized from fifty years ago. "That's the first intelligent thing you've said all day." Then she squeaked her cart down the aisle, away from him.

6

*I*t wasn't that, in her forty years as an ACLU
lawyer, Chris had never found herself on her knees.
Quite the contrary. It was just that she had never
enjoyed it before.

She knelt in her garden, crawled and dug, allowing
herself to get as dirty as she had at four years old,
making mudpies in her parents' backyard in Brooklyn.
She was plucking and bulbing, inhaling the scent of the
turned earth as appreciatively as she inhaled a good
bordeaux. Karen was nearby, painting a scene from
their backyard, the focal point of which was their
birdbath, which so far was attracting more squirrels
than mockingbirds.

Chris turned and sat in the dirt; this is what was
required these days, she had discovered, in order to

get up from an extended period of crouching. Her knees locked and stretching her legs back out too fast was, when it wasn't impossible, excruciating. This way, she sat down, her butt in full contact with the soft earth, and let her legs unreel slowly. She had learned over the last few years to be patient with her body. It was a little like the sensation you had trying to run underwater; your mind knew what it wanted your body to do, but your body was helpless to go any faster.

She sat, waiting for the feeling to return to her calves, and watched Karen, her hand moving in painstaking slow-motion over the canvas. They were together three years, a long time for Chris, but nearly newlyweds compared to most of their friends. Angie and Ruth were together twelve years, the guys twenty, and Lara and Helen a breathtaking thirty-five.

But it still amazed her that she and Karen were together at all. After all, when they'd met, Karen was married. What's more, she was married to the man Chris was trying to discredit to the tune of a million dollars in a class-action suit brought by three black employees who'd accused him of cutting off their careers at the knees when they worked at his paper plant. After Chris won, Karen had turned up at her office the next day and asked her to lunch. She announced over the meal that she'd come to the conclusion, after watching the trial for weeks, that of all the people in the courtroom the one she least wanted to be associated with was her husband and the one she most wanted to be associated with was Chris. When, after a month of intense friendship, Chris told her she was a lesbian, Karen had said, "Do I need to be a lesbian, too, to be in love with you?" Three months later Karen had left her newly bankrupt husband and moved in with Chris.

When she was finally upright again, Chris wandered over and watched Karen from a few yards away, wanting to be closer to her but not daring to disturb her. Chris had been one of those people on whom singleness had been wasted. Her mated friends wistfully expressed the desire to change places with her, for just a month at a time, but she had never seen the life's charms. Dating a new woman every six months registered with her only as failure, not joyful variety; not having to be monogamous was a disappointment, not a delight. And yet, the thing she wanted for so long — a happy marriage — had always eluded her. In its place, she had had to settle for dating a parade of women who had been neurotic, deceitful, shallow, crazy, cruel, depressed, and phobic. It had frightened her, after a while, that there were so many disturbed people loose on the streets.

Karen turned and smiled. She had her honey-colored hair pulled back into a stubby ponytail, and her long, paint-splattered smock covered everything but her slender neck at one end and her shapely calves at the other. She shifted barefoot on the grass and ran the back of her hand across her forehead.

"All this exercise," she said, "makes a girl work up a sweat."

Chris smiled back, happy to be acknowledged, to be invited to approach. She still had to guard against the tendency to smother Karen.

"It's really coming to life," Chris said, surveying the canvas. For days, it had seemed all wispy watercolor brush strokes to her, with no particular image threatening to emerge. Now she could see the birdbath, the family of cardinals swirling around it; she could even sense their motion, see the quality of the early morning sun washing over everything. "You know, I think this is really very good. I think this may be a breakthrough."

"You're sweet," Karen said, studying her work, too.

"No, no," Chris said, taking her elbow. "I'm not trying to butter you up. I think this is going to be exceptional."

Karen grinned. "I think you mean it."

"I do. I do. Finish it. Go on," Chris said, urgent now. She felt she must go away, not trespass anymore on the chemistry between Karen and the canvas. Because that was the last thing she ever wanted to do, demand Karen's attention if she wasn't earning it naturally.

7

*R*udy was driving the Lexus slowly, as slowly as one of the white heads — as he still called them, to Rich's chagrin, now that he was silver-haired himself. He was scanning for the ideal storefront. He didn't want one of these horrid little strip malls with their Eckerds and Kmarts. He needed a location with more class, something that announced uncommon quality, at least for these parts. As for the name, he was going to keep it simple: Rudy's Catering. Nothing too challenging to remember — important, considering the aged clientele — and since he planned to answer the phone himself, his goal was to have his first name become as well known as Charo's or Frankie's, or whoever it was down here who passed for a superstar.

He had eaten his way through the immediate area and had decided that, without a doubt, he could make a small fortune trouncing the competition. Never had he tasted so much mushy pasta, stringy vegetables, rubbery chicken and boring bread in such a concentrated period of time. But in truth, money was not his motivation — and God knew, with their new tax status as retirees, whether that would even pose more problems. Mostly, it was self-defense. If he was not able to buy the kind of food he considered palatable, he was going to have to cook it himself.

A restaurant was out of the question, though. He hadn't retired so he could be a slave to a business, night and day. Catering would be much more manageable, since he could control how much work he'd have by putting a cap on the number of orders he'd take. And given how cheap everything (and every*one*) was down here, he could easily hire a cook or even two to help. Rich would do the books, of course, since all that number-crunching stuff that gave him such a hard-on. And thank God for that, because he himself hated it.

Rudy's tastes — in food and in men — ran to French and Greek. So he planned some specials like beef bourguignon, lamb stew with couscous, moussaka with eggplant. But to cater well he knew he needed standards like a lemon ginger chicken breast dish, vegetable lasagne, sole with red potatoes. Yes, yes, he was going to make a tasty profit indeed!

Besides, it was for the best for him and Rich. If anything about two men being together for life was unnatural, it was only this: they could not be idle. They could not sit across a living room day after day, admiring the slant of the sunlight, reminiscing about trips and tricks gone by. No, men were active creatures, they needed to be in motion, and in his own case, *com*motion was even better.

8

*N*apping was what Helen feared most. That's how she remembered her own mother's life for the last five years of it: one long napfest. Nodding off — her head at some unlikely angle — and starting awake, her chin quaking with the effort. And, her mother had told her, there were intense dreams about some regret or mistake she'd made in her life, very fresh and close to the surface, retrievable, unlike night dreams, which were so deeply lodged that their dark colors and dark truths could rarely be excavated.

So when Helen was facing down that long runway of afternoon, she kept on watch for the desire to doze. As soon as she felt its warm lapping pull, she'd bolt from the chair, leash up Emma, and head out the door.

They'd walked a good three-quarters of a mile —

Helen knew because she wore an odometer — when she heard the low hum of a golf cart gaining on them from behind. "Yoo hoo!" a woman's voice called out, and Emma whirled around protectively. It was Felicia Olson. Helen scratched Emma behind the ear to let the dog know all was well. Emma immediately relaxed, and wagged her tail in a long, slow sweep as the cart, bearing Felicia in a paisley sun dress, puttered to a stop alongside them.

"Nice to see you again, Felicia," Helen said. "Do you remember Emma?"

"Certainly I do," Felicia said. "I see you two walk straight past my house nearly every day, nearly the same time, too, somewhere between three and four. You ought to get yourself one of these golf carts to travel around in. We all have them. It's a lot easier on the old peds."

"I'm sure," Helen said. "But Emma would find it an unfair advantage."

Felicia laughed, and it made her small-featured, narrow face seem briefly younger. "It'd please me if you both stopped into my place this time for a cup of fresh coffee — and a bowl of water, of course."

Helen agreed and Felicia, going lightly on the gas pedal, narrated as they went. She pointed out the houses, nearly identical except for the color of the trim or the placement of bushes, and told Helen who lived in them. "A widow from Maine" or "a dentist and his wife from Delaware" were mainly how people were described. It gave Helen a chill. Everyone was known for his or her life *before* Lakeside Leisure. No one seemed to have distinguished herself down here. Helen could almost feel the houses inhaling and exhaling, idling, dozing.

As they rounded a corner, the houses changed abruptly. They were smaller, low-slung ranches. There were no spanish-tile roofs, no fancy landscaping.

"This is the first phase of the community," Felicia explained. "Before it got so grand."

Felicia parked her golf cart under the car port and unlocked the front door. "Is Emma invited in?" Helen asked. "Not everyone wants a dog —"

"Don't think twice about it. Of course she's welcome."

The house was shadowy, almost as though the windows were too low to catch the light, and the room's dark wood and maroon plaid couches didn't help brighten it up. Still, it was cozy with framed photos and a long, rectangular fish tank, its water streaked with flashes of fast-moving violet, ruby and amber fish. Helen scanned the photos and quickly figured that Felicia had two grown sons, both married, one to a black woman, a fact that both surprised Helen and gave her hope; maybe no family was as conventional as it seemed from a distance. "It's very homey," Helen said, smiling. Emma, curling up immediately in front of a recliner, seemed to agree.

"Thank you. How do you take your coffee?" Felicia called in from the kitchen.

"Black, no sugar."

Felicia was back in seconds.

"How'd you get that so fast?" Helen asked.

"Oh, Ted and I keep a pot brewing all the time. Ted, especially, has a cup in his hand nearly all day. I'd introduce him but he's not here just now. What did you say your husband's name was?"

A rod of tension shot down Helen's neck and into

both shoulders. She felt bad because Felicia had not meant to walk into this quicksand of intimacy. It was such an easy social question, the most innocent, routine even, among heterosexuals. Helen looked into Felicia's pale round face, creased with tiny wrinkles the way a newborn's feet are, and tried in vain to think of some way to spare her.

"You're right, I didn't say," Helen said. "No, I didn't say. Because, uh, I don't have a husband."

"Oh, I'm sorry, dear," Felicia said, frowning. "I didn't realize you were widowed. I thought you'd said something that day we talked . . . something that made me think your husband was still alive."

"Well, ah, what I said was 'my partner.' " Helen got up to pace. Emma sprang to all fours, anticipating departure. "Lay down, Emma, stay," Helen said, and the dog obeyed.

"Oh, stupid me, again," Felicia said. "I keep assuming everyone is married. You're easily ten years younger than me. I know these days people divorce and they don't always remarry. And living together makes good financial sense at our age. I understand completely, yes, yes, I do," Felicia finished up, nodding and sipping, clearly agitated.

"Well, yes, that's right. There are all kinds of different arrangements." In her head, Helen imagined Angie and Ruth admonishing her, urging her to say outright what her life was. Instead, she asked Felicia about each of the pictures, learning her children and grandchildren's names, where they lived and what they did, how often she saw them and how often they visited. Helen envied her, the way she had envied others a million times in her life, the ease with which they could discuss their families, wear them on their sleeves, boast even, without first measuring the amount of alienation it might cost.

"Listen, this has been a very nice visit but I have to be heading back," Helen said. "Heel, Emma," she commanded, and the dog was instantly at her ankle.

"I swear that dog can sense when your breathing changes," Felicia marveled.

"She's a love," Helen said, patting the dog heartily on her rump. The two of them were nearly home free, Helen noted, when Felicia spoke.

"But here I go again, a mind like a sieve. What's the name of your gentleman? I mean to invite you both to dinner. Ted'll want to know who he'll be talking to."

"Oh — that's sweet," Helen said. "Lara, tell him." And then she and Emma broke into a trot.

9

*F*or fifteen minutes, Georgia Novack watched the attractive woman circling her gallery, pausing appreciatively in front of the spotlighted oils, lingering in front of the watercolors, before she considered approaching her. Georgia could spot a potential buyer from the slow and studied stride, the intent, sober expression, when she saw one.

Flattery, she found, always worked well. "Are you a painter yourself?" Georgia asked the woman, taking in her designer jade shorts-and-sweater set, registering that this was someone with style and the money to express it.

"Oh, well, yes, I suppose, as a matter of fact I am," the woman said, barely glancing away from the still life she had stopped in front of.

Oh, great, Georgia thought to herself. Just what she needed, another artist wanna-be. What she really needed was someone hopeless who leaned toward pretension in her decorating taste. "Well, it takes an artist to appreciate art, I feel," Georgia managed.

A pale blush came to the woman's smooth, ivory cheek. In fact, her skin — not yet over-tanned and thatched with wrinkles — gave her away as both new to town and younger than most.

"Any favorites?" Georgia asked, not sure yet how she was going to direct her sales pitch.

"Look, I really don't mean to waste your time. I'm just browsing —"

"No, I really just want to know," Georgia said, realizing suddenly that she was genuinely curious.

"Well, okay. Over here." The woman walked ahead and led the way into one of Georgia's recessed rooms, stopping in front of a small oil of a hummingbird mid-flight, against a strange, red sky. Most of Georgia's customers never gave it a second glance, since it wasn't the right size or scene to make a room, and yet Georgia knew it was absolutely the finest piece of artwork in her gallery. And it was one of her own favorites, too, which was partly why she kept it unremarkably displayed way in the back, half hoping no one would ever want it, so she could keep it forever by default.

"I could probably get you a good price on it," Georgia said, her commercial instincts overcoming her sentiment. "It's one of my best pieces but I confess it's been with me a while. Frankly a lot of people down here are looking for wall decorations, not fine art, and I think it's wasted on most of my customers."

"Who is the artist?"

"A local woman," Georgia said. "She's dead over ten years now. Her name was Lee-Ann Hollyock. Eccentric. Lived alone as far as anyone could tell. Sold only a few paintings in her lifetime, all birds, but I keep track of them. They've all appreciated nicely, so her work really is an investment."

The woman leaned closer. "You would swear the bird is moving in front of your eyes. It couldn't have been easy to paint. She would have had to memorize the movement, keep seeing it exactly in her head, while she painted. Because you don't get a humming-bird to pose for you."

"No, I bet you're right about that," Georgia said, laughing lightly. The two of them stood side by side and regarded the painting. "I'm Georgia Novack, by the way," she said after a moment. "I own the gallery. Nice to meet you."

"Karen Barth."

"You keep browsing, and let me know if you need any other information." Georgia smiled and started to walk away, trying to shrug off the impulse of what she wanted to say next. "And um, if you ever have any of your own work that you think you might consider selling, let me see it."

"Oh, well, that's very kind, thank you," the woman said, this time blushing brightly.

Usually it was a disaster to make that kind of invitation. The work was invariably awful, and then you'd alienated a customer for good — not to mention her circle of friends. But Georgia had a hunch this time could be different. And sometimes you just had to play your hunches.

10

*N*ow, I do not want you blowing this opportunity," Bunny Seagirt was lecturing Felicia.

"What opportunity would that be, Bunny? All I said is I'm having two of the new neighbors over for dinner."

They were on Bunny's backyard deck, under a white umbrella, sipping unsweetened iced tea.

"You know very well what opportunity I mean," Bunny said, fluffing her gauzy floral skirt in front of her on the lounge chair. It irked Bunny how Felicia was always trying to take the high road, always trying to make her feel the moral equivalent of a gnat, when the truth was, without Bunny's no-nonsense vigilance, Lakeside Leisure would not still be as thriving a community as it was.

"You mean you want me to grill them," Felicia said.

"All I would like is to know that they are our kind of people," Bunny said. "You're having Helen and — what's her husband's name?"

"Well, I don't think for sure it's her husband, but I'm pretty sure she said his name is Larry."

"So there you go. First find out why they're not married."

"I will *not* ask them that, Bunny. It's nobody's beeswax, least of all ours."

Bunny scowled as she watched Felicia dab at her forehead with her perfumed handkerchief. "And why is that, Felicia? Because our property values are not at stake? Because the reputation of the whole community is not upheld house by house? Because every last dime of my savings is not sunk into this slice of Florida and I don't want any sex-crazed, wife-swapping, French-kissing radicals making this place a mecca for weirdos? Is that why?"

Felicia peeked out over the top of her sunglasses. "Are you suggesting I ask them that before or *after* the appetizers?"

"Go ahead, make fun, Felicia," Bunny said, folding her arms. "But don't come crying to me when they're having psychedelic drug parties on their front lawn and inviting Ted to join in."

Felicia burst out laughing. "Bunny, your imagination really is wasted on this place. Why would people who want to behave like that move to little old Lakeside Leisure?"

"For the same reasons we did, Felicia. Because it's beautiful and peaceful and you can get good value for your dollar and —"

"Exactly, Bunny. Pretty unlikely that it was listed as

a hospitable setting for psycho sex orgies or whatever you call them."

"Oh, don't be so naive, Felicia," Bunny said, swatting a wasp away from her sweating glass of iced tea. "That's what they like to do—quietly infiltrate some unsuspecting neighborhood where they think nobody will be on to them. I saw it once on *Geraldo*."

"Well, you'll be the first to know, Bunny, if they suggest a sex swap by dessert."

"You do that, Felicia. You let me know exactly everything they say." Because, Bunny knew, unless she got a direct transcript, she couldn't trust Felicia not to miss the point.

11

*R*uth knew that Angie wasn't so much interested in actually being a Lakeside Leisure clubhouse member as much as she was in the act of joining.

The flyer was what had first gotten Angie's attention. Left rolled in their mailbox tied with a red "Welcome, New Neighbors" ribbon, it regaled the benefits of the clubhouse, which included a health club, pool, tennis courts, and priority tee times at the golf course. The fee was $1,000 a year per person, or $1,500 per couple. Angie had come running into the living room, thrusting the flyer at Ruth, and shouting about how she was going to call and dare them to tell her who qualified as a couple.

Ruth had watched her agitated lover storming

around the room. She knew that Angie needed to periodically make herself conspicuous to the larger world, and she knew, too, that she was still boiling over the supermarket masher who'd tried to pick her up. That meant that this particular display of hetero-sexuality was not going to go unpunished. Seeing that she was going to be recruited for insurrection whether she liked it or not, Ruth had decided to try to convince Angie of a more moderate course.

The day they went to the clubhouse, they smiled together at the rotund woman behind the semicircular desk. The woman smiled back, her eyes crinkling into slits. Ice blue hair, not unlike cotton candy, swirled atop her head.

"We'd like an application," Ruth said evenly.

"Of course, dearie, and welcome. I know you're going to just *love* it here. New to these parts?"

"Yes. From Manhattan," Ruth said, in anticipation of what was always the standard next question.

The woman slid an application form at each of them — Angie kicked the side of Ruth's shoe in alarm — smiling her slit-eye smile again. "And where did you move down from? Oh, silly me, you just said so. Gee whiz, Manhattan. I'll bet you're relieved to be out of there!"

"There'll be plenty of things we'll miss, actually," Ruth said, warily eyeing Angie who was furiously scribbling her way through her form.

"Oh, my, city slickers, are you?" The woman laughed, making a kind of snorting sound. Ruth was starting to feel bad that this woman was going to have to be the target of their protest; Ruth did not have the

42

same kind of free-floating rage Angie did. "What kind of work did your husbands do?"

"No husbands —"

"Oh, I'm *so* sorry, dear," the woman said.

"Don't be," Ruth said.

"Oh!"

"No, no — there were never any. But Angie and I, since you asked, are both doctors. I'm a gynecologist and Angie's a Ph.D. English, modernism."

"Oooh, a lady gynecologist. That wouldn't be for me, no. I couldn't go to another lady for, you know, things of that nature."

"Actually —"

"Here's our form," Angie interrupted. "And a check for fifteen hundred dollars."

"Okay, let's see here," the woman said, hoisting onto her nose the pair of glasses that dangled from a chain around her neck.

"Naplestein, Angie and Ruth," she read. "Oh, you're sisters. That's so nice. But it's just a thousand for one of you. And you both need to fill out a separate form." She shoved the one that was in front of Ruth a little closer to her.

"No, we're not sisters, not the kind you're thinking of, anyway," Angie said. This time, Ruth kicked the heel of Angie's shoe in warning. They had agreed they would be polite, not snide.

"We're applying as a couple," Ruth said, affecting her most modulated doctor's voice. The tone implied: Please reconsider reality from the correct point of view — mine.

The woman tugged her glasses off her nose. "Oh,

but dear, if you're sisters, you don't qualify for the couple rate. That's only for a husband and wife, one household, you know. Otherwise, we'd have all the widows teaming up in here to get the five hundred dollar discount." She laughed again.

"We're not sisters. We're a couple, one household," Ruth said. "Naplestein is our combined last name — legally changed, by the way. So unless you tell us that the clubhouse's policy is discriminatory against same-sex couples, then we qualify the same way a heterosexual couple qualifies."

The woman's jaw dropped, her mouth making a little "O" like a donut hole. She folded her arms across her chest and seemed to keep trying to wrap herself more tightly, finally hugging her shoulders, her arms over her chest like scissors. "Are you trying to tell me that you two are a pair of—" and here she lowered her voice to a butterscotch-scented whisper — *"lesbians?"*

"Yes, we're a pair of lesbians," Angie said loudly. There was a high-C shriek behind them and Ruth turned around in time to see two old women collide and fall on top of each other on the carpet in a heap, their four dimpled thighs flailing in the air. Ruth rushed over and helped them to their feet. Once righted, they scurried off like cockroaches in a suddenly well-lit room.

Ruth walked back over to the desk, where Angie was beaming at her. The blue-haired woman was glaring. "And you were a gynecologist? That's just *perverted,*" she said.

"Are you going to process our application as a couple or not?" Ruth asked.

"Absolutely not," the woman said, her neck jiggling

now with righteous indignation. "I don't know what couple means up there in Manhattan, but down here, it means a man and a wife, in the eyes of the church and the state."

"Fine. You'll hear from our lawyer, then," Ruth said. "And you can tell your boss that this is going to be the first application that cost *him* money."

And they walked out, as planned, hand in hand.

12

*B*ill Seagirt was more accustomed to being the straddler than the straddlee, but since it was Sissy Armonk who was on top of him, he had no complaint. Sissy Armonk, with her perfect, brand new 38 double C bosom was riding him with the abandon of a child playing horsey on her daddy's knee.

When he came, he roared — not so much with ecstasy as with relief, since screwing these days took so long — and he nearly pitched her off the bed with his bucking. Luckily he caught her by the arm just in time. "Whoa there, girl," he said, registering her torso's soft rolls of skin, loose as chiffon — everywhere, that was, except for her breasts, which jutted out in front of her like refrigerator shelves, Mazda headlights, camel humps.

"Oh, Billy, you are a silver stud," Sissy said, throwing herself on her back on the pile of pillows.

He hated her to call him "Billy" but all his corrections and objections fell on deaf ears. Literally, because she took out her hearing aid during sex. He never asked her why she removed it but he suspected she was afraid of somehow getting electrocuted. That left her eighty percent deaf in her right ear. She was only sixty-five years old, but you never knew, past sixty, which part of your chassis was going to drop right out on the street underneath you. He was sixty-seven himself and in good health, and yet he had learned not to gloat.

He lay on his side, facing her, pillows rolled like logs under his armpits. "I hope you were using protection, because I wasn't," he whispered once she put her hearing aid back in. "That's all we'd need is for you to get pregnant."

She laughed, barely stirring her breasts, which were pointed at the ceiling like rockets on a launch pad. "Yes, one of the few pleasures of old age," she said, her voice getting that dreamy lilt it got whenever she was going to get maudlin on him. "I am so lucky to have you," she said, cupping his face in her hands. "Of course, I don't *really* have you," she said, pulling away.

"Sure you do, Sissy," he said. "You know, at our age, we're all on borrowed time, anyway."

"Oh, go on," she said, shoving him playfully. "You're strong as an ox. You'll live thirty more years."

"We'll have all the time together we need," he said, already itching for a good golf game with the guys. His whole life, he had never relished mooning around on the sheets with a woman after the deed was done, and he wasn't about to start now. He got up and retrieved his neatly folded clothes from the floral wing chair beside the bed.

"Do you love Bunny?" Sissy asked. She was on her side, the sheet pulled up to just under her breasts.

He stepped into his boxers and considered one of the time-honored lines he might use: "Not like I love you, honey." But that wasn't an option since they hadn't said any "I love yous" yet. There was also "Yes, but more like a sister these days." Or the ever trusty, "Yes, but I'm not *in* love." But he'd been down most of those roads, and while they worked well in the short run, in the long run they always led to more trouble. In his experience, women built elaborate psychological traps around them, eventually using his own words to argue with lawyer-like precision the folly and treachery of his behavior. He had never before considered telling any of them the truth.

"Billy, did you hear me?" Sissy asked.

I'm not the one who's deaf, he thought to say but stopped himself. "I heard you, Sissy. I just don't see why it should matter to you if I love Bunny or not."

"You don't think it matters?" He heard the beginnings of the quiver in her voice.

"I didn't say that," he said, pulling on his socks. "I said I don't see that it has to matter to *you*. It doesn't change anything between us. Do you think that if I didn't love Bunny, I would therefore love you more, and get divorced? At sixty-seven? And what if I do love Bunny? I'm still here with you, so what good does my loving her do?" He stood there, feeling lightheaded, buckling his belt, watching her face go pasty white. He hadn't thought about these things before, not consciously, but now that he was saying them, he felt emboldened. "I've slept with lots of women in my life, Sissy. Some people would say that means I've loved lots. Others would say it means I've loved none. People judge a man like me different ways."

Sissy grabbed one of the pillows and began to sob into it, making a muffled, underwater sound, like she was trying to suffocate herself.

He sat, shirtless, on the edge of the bed. "Sissy, pull that pillow away. I'm just trying to be honest," he said, but as soon as he wrested the pillow from her, she covered her face with her hands.

"You're just taking advantage of an old divorcee like me," she said through her tears. "Men always have the better deal in life — at twenty, at forty, at sixty. Women don't ever catch up."

"How do you know you're not taking advantage of me, Sissy?"

"Who do you think I got these things for?" she said, sitting up suddenly, grabbing her breasts. "Do you think I like rolling on my stomach in the middle of the night and feeling like I've got a life preserver strapped to my rib cage? Huh?" Her face was salmon-colored with rage.

"Look, Sissy —"

"I got them for Everett, that's who. As a present for his fiftieth birthday. And he left me the next year for our landscaper, a girl who was barely older than our own *daughter*! That's what women are always doing, worrying about what makes their men happy. And men — they're always either lying or being brutally honest. Haven't any of you figured out yet that none of that has anything to do with making a woman happy?"

He was scared now. He wondered what she was

capable of. Next time, he promised himself, he'd stick with "Not as much as I love you, honey." He shrugged into his shirt as he headed out through the living room to the front door.

13

*L*ara was not happy — and she hadn't for a moment all day let Helen forget it.

At first she had refused to go to dinner at Felicia and Ted's, since it had been arranged, she felt, under false pretenses. But then Helen had argued that they'd only be postponing the inevitable, that sooner or later the neighbors were going to find out the houses in Paxton Court were not arranged boy-girl, boy-girl, and she refused to be a prisoner of her own backyard forestalling that revelation. (Angie had suggested telling them the houses were butch-femme, butch- femme, but Helen had pointedly ignored her.) Besides, Helen reminded her, she had said Lara's name to Felicia on the way out and she thought it was fair to assume that Felicia had registered that it was female name.

Lara knew there was no point in arguing further, but that didn't stop her from doing so. All day long she protested and needled Helen, not because she was afraid of confronting anyone about her life, but because she was tired of socializing with people out of obligation, and an elderly straight couple was not at the top of her list of people she was eager to break the ice with.

"You know, we're an elderly queer couple, so I wouldn't go putting on airs," Helen had said, fixing her makeup in the bathroom mirror.

"You don't look elderly to me," Lara said, scooting up behind Helen and nuzzling her neck. And she didn't feel elderly herself, especially when it came to her desire for Helen.

"You're just stalling again, Lara," Helen had said, kissing her on the nose. "Go get yourself dressed."

So that's how they ended up on Felicia and Ted's doorstep, against Lara's better instincts.

Felicia answered the door, smiling and looking scrubbed and starched in a pink-and-white striped dress. She was glancing nervously past them, down the steps, as if she were expecting someone else. "Oh, is something wrong, dear, that Larry couldn't make it?" she asked.

"Larry? Who's . . . oh! Felicia, this is Lara. Lara is my partner. Did you think I said Larry?"

Lara aimed at Helen the most I-told-you-so, you-owe-me-big-time glare she could manage, but Helen was avoiding her eyes.

"Oh, stupid me," Felicia said. "I'm always bollixing something up. Well, come on in, now, please. Ted," she called ahead, "come on and meet Helen and Lara. That's Lara, Ted — not Larry, silly old me."

A short, shuffling man emerged from the shadows of the living room, his gray hair loose and wiry like a burst Brillo pad, his glasses thick and prominent on his face. "Pleased, I'm sure," he said, putting out his hand. "So what happened? Larry couldn't make it?"

Helen and Felicia matched each other's high-pitched laugh, while Lara and Ted regarded each other blankly.

"No, Ted. Lara is Helen's friend's name. I only *thought* she said Larry. Now why don't we sit down at the table — dinner's just about ready."

Felicia hustled into the kitchen, leaving Ted to seat everyone. Lara kept scowling at Helen across the table till she caught her eye, and then she frowned hard, her signal that they were to get through this meal as quickly as possible and then leave. Helen merely pursed her lips, meaning, Lara knew, that they were at a stalemate.

"Can I help you out there, Felicia?" Helen called.

"Oh, no, here I come," Felicia said, gripping with red checkered oven mitts a steaming pot of spaghetti topped with meatballs, sausage and peppers.

"It smells wonderful," Lara said, suddenly feeling a burning need to establish herself, to assert that she was not somehow Larry in drag.

"Dig in, everyone," Felicia said, sweating slightly. Lara couldn't judge whether it was from nerves or exertion. It had been a long time, Lara realized, when she'd simply arrived at someone's house and sat down to the main meal. Her whole adult work life had been filled with meals eaten during a kind of dance: first the cocktails and hors d'oeuvres balanced on your palm or knee for an hour, then appetizers and salads and breads, all long before anything like an entree arrived.

And by that time you were stuffed and exhausted. She decided she liked Felicia's straightforward style.

Ted took control of the conversation. Like many men, Lara noted, he calmly assumed he himself was a worthy topic of exclusive discussion, and he described his years as a post office manager, and why he thought service had fallen off so badly recently. "But I guess the only professionals people complain about more than postal workers are lawyers, wouldn't you say, girls?" he asked.

Lara was happy to oblige with horror stories about furious clients and cases gone wrong, and soon they were all full and friendly. Lara was amazed to see it so easily accomplished. Here she had been ready to wall herself away, sure that her neighbors wouldn't be able to look the lesbians-next-door in the eye.

"So how can it be that such lovely ladies like yourselves never married?" Ted asked, pushing back from the table and stretching his legs. He rubbed his hands contentedly on his stomach.

"Ted!" Felicia squealed. "What a question!"

"Why?" he asked, genuinely stumped, Lara realized. All this while, all these stories she and Helen had been telling about what was clearly an entire life spent side by side, and still he hadn't put the picture together. All her life she'd seen people do that: they saw only what confirmed their beliefs and biases, and they made the most outlandish rationalizations to accommodate that, to keep them blind to reality. That was always the struggle with seating juries, because some people would just always find the cop guilty of brutality, or conclude that the woman was asking to be raped, or say the high-paid exec was definitely ripping off the company. Evidence was a weak antidote to such powerful prejudices. She locked eyes with Helen across the table, trying to telegraph that handling Ted was completely her call. Like a hundred other times in their lives, here was the choice: laugh it off, smooth it over, blame careers or bad luck or bad dates for a life without marriage. Or, disrupt a perfectly amiable evening with the rupture of coming out.

"Oh, well, Ted, we are married," Helen said slowly. Lara watched her admiringly across the table, her stomach dipping with fear nonetheless. This place was their new home and she realized in that moment how much she wanted to be welcome. "We're married to each other, Lara and I. Not legally, of course, but in every other way."

Lara held her breath and stared into her plate. Felicia and Ted were only about ten years older, and yet she felt between them an entire generational divide.

"I hope we haven't upset you," Helen said into the spaghetti-sauce scented silence.

"Oh, no, no, no," Felicia said, a little breathlessly, as if she had just run a marathon. "No, no, no, no. What's to be upset about? You're both lovely people. I'm just—just sorry if we made it awkward for you." She reached over and patted Helen's hand.

Another throat-clearing silence followed. Lara, desperate to hold up her end of things, tried in vain to think of something to say.

"Well, it makes no difference to me," Ted said gravely. "But I just hope somebody's told Larry."

14

*T*hrough her telescope, Bunny had seen Helen and another person — a womanly-looking person — leave the lavender Paxton Court house and return three hours later. As soon as she saw the front door close behind them, she was on the phone to Felicia.

"Felicia, who was that with Helen? Was that a woman? What happened to Larry?"

"Well, hi, Bunny, and how are you?" Felicia asked. "Surveying the stars again this evening?"

Bunny heard the droll sarcasm, and she was not amused. "We had a deal, Felicia. Now what went on over there at your dinner party?"

"*We* didn't have a deal, Bunny. *You* had a delusion."

"Felicia, how can you speak to me like that? I am one of your oldest friends!"

"Well it's certainly true that you're old, Bunny."

"Felicia, what has gotten into you?" Bunny didn't give a gnat's turd about any kind of sisterhood with Felicia, but for the moment she needed her, and playing the role of wounded friend seemed the most promising route to take.

"Bunny, if you want to get to know them, have them over to dinner yourself."

"That means you know something you're not telling me. What are you not telling me, Felicia? What happened to Larry?"

"Not Larry. Lara. I heard wrong."

"Lara! So it *was* a woman I saw. Helen lives with another woman? What do you suppose that means?" Bunny was getting a bad feeling.

"That they agree on wallpaper and there's no fights over the toilet seat."

"*Felicia!* It's just like you to miss the nuances."

"Agreeing on wallpaper is not a nuance."

Bunny shivered with impatience; Felicia could not be trusted with the simplest missions. "Well, *I* don't like what I think it means. Because *I* think it means they're lesbians. *Dykes.* Oh, *God!* What are we going to do?"

"Bunny, how can they be lesbians if Helen is having an affair with the man at the end of the block?"

"Good Lord, she *told* you that?"

"No, *you* told me that."

"Well, maybe I was wrong."

"Exactly," Felicia said.

Bunny hated her smug, imperious tone. "There are

facts here, Felicia. Fact one: Helen lives with this Lara person. They've retired together. Now, you may be naive, Felicia, but I don't think that means they're bridge buddies."

"Well, I like them both a lot, Bunny, and I don't care if they're bridge buddies or, or — bosom buddies!"

"Oh, really? Well, you will. Do you think those kind of people live like we do, Felicia? You'll see — and too late — that they don't have the same morals as we do. They'll be preaching special rights and free sex and starting all kinds of orgy clubs and — Good Lord — let's keep them away from the *children!*"

"What children, Bunny? This is a retirement village, for God's sake."

"We all have children who visit, Felicia, you and I both."

"Bunny, my children are thirty years old."

"Thirteen, thirty — what's the difference? They're still our *ba*bies! Oh, Lord, I tell you, this could be our downfall! But I won't let it happen. I won't. I'm not going to let their perversion pollute our happy homes!"

"Bunny, you worry about your home — I'll worry about mine."

"See, Felicia — they've brainwashed you already!"

15

*W*hat are you talking about, sue the clubhouse?" Chris asked. She had woken up only fifteen minutes earlier, and was still in her purple silk robe, her eyes puffy, her stomach empty. Angie had turned up on the doorstep and barged into the living room, trailing complaints as she went, relaying a tale of being refused a couple membership at the club and promising to sue for discrimination. "Couldn't I just whip you up an omelette instead of a lawsuit?" Chris asked, trying to coax Angie by the elbow into the kitchen.

"Look, Chris, this is about all of us, not just me and Ruth."

"I know that, I know that," Chris said, encouraged that she'd steered Angie to one of the kitchen bar stools. She popped an English muffin into the toaster. "But you know, I'm retired now, remember? We all are."

"And you're willing to retire your sense of right and wrong at the same time?" Angie asked.

Chris sighed. She wondered how Angie had the energy to be politically correct seven days a week. For herself, she had at least taken the weekends off. "Of course not. I just think you should get a lawyer who's actually still practicing." She blinked painfully into the sun that was streaming in through the sliding glass doors. A dull band of headache was wrapping itself around her skull.

"Chris, be real. Who am I supposed to call down here?"

"I'm sure Lambda Legal Defense can give you a referral." Chris was finding it hard to look directly at Angie. Angie was too aggressively awake and it was hurting Chris's eyes.

"Look, we both realize this is not gays in the military," Angie said. "It's just plain old dykes in the clubhouse. Not exactly a reputation maker."

"Exactly — and you're talking about a fifty dollar discount here."

"Five hundred. And besides, where are your ACLU instincts? We're talking about a principle."

"It's very hard to regulate private clubs."

"*I want you to sue them,*" Angie said, stressing every word. "I'll pay you whatever you ask."

"Angie, it's not the money —"

"You just said it *was* the money!"

The muffin popped up out of the toaster with a clatter of springs. The toasty smell of impending sustenance made Chris more conciliatory. "Okay, look, tell you what. I'll write them a letter on my legal letterhead. But that's it—"

Angie had already thrown her arms around Chris's neck and was kissing her.

"*Ahem,*" Karen said, suddenly appearing in the kitchen doorway.

Chris instinctively jumped away. "Honey, it's not what it looks like."

"I know," Karen said, waving away Chris's protests. "For a minute, it looked like two lesbians kissing in my kitchen."

"I think I've just been hired as Angie and Ruth's lawyer."

"I hope that's not your method of payment, Angie," Karen said.

"Oh no," Angie said. "If it were, I'd be expecting something a lot better than a lawsuit."

16

*A*s far as Rich Dubrow was concerned, one needed to be cut out for retirement; not everyone was good at it. His circle of friends were so far very bad at it. No one quite had the knack for it that he did. Angie and Ruth were still crusading, Lara and Chris felt lost without Important Work, Karen seemed to have found her calling as a painter all of a sudden, and his own beloved couldn't relax under threat of divorce. Rudy's catering business was open only a week and already he'd had three jobs and had to hire a woman to help with the cooking.

Rich, on the other hand, knew himself to be supremely suited to leisure. The secret to a happy retirement, he had discovered, was to have loathed your work your whole life — which fortunately he had.

He hadn't even realized how much until he'd stopped doing it. It wasn't just the constant glad-handing and deal-making and soul-selling, but all the lying: The dinners out with clients, dragging along some hapless date, or having to go solo, boozing it up as one of the guys and having to talk like a playboy. Sure, some people suspected the truth about him after a while, but that just made things even more absurd, because it didn't mean he could drop the heterosexual charade; it just meant that then he felt all that more ridiculous and counterfeit doing it. All the press attention that the military "don't ask, don't tell" policy had gotten galled him; it was how most gay people had lived their work lives for decades, and it hadn't ever made the front page of any newspaper before.

The fact that he'd made more money than his entire extended family put together hadn't made his work one drop sweeter. Yes, he had liked—no, adored—what the money had bought him: the vacations abroad, the wardrobe, the cars, the orchestra seats. And most of these had been acquired tastes; he had had to grow into his earning power. For instance, he had always admired fine cars from afar, the way you'd marvel at an exotic bird flying by, but he had not necessarily felt that he actually had to *own* one. But eventually he got over that, had gone from grateful to taking-for-granted.

He had been ambivalent, too, about the power—ambivalent because he had discovered that he could never really feel he was "off," never really feel he could stop worrying if the people he and Rudy were chatting with during the play intermission, or next to them at the sushi bar, were potential clients. In the end he must have liked it enough to put up with what was essentially a loss of freedom and privacy. All the while, he didn't doubt that if he had ever glimpsed some other kind of work that promised even a modicum of pleasure, he would have switched. But he never did.

The truth was, he had made so much money, he and Rudy could have retired anywhere in the *world* and been comfortable, but Helen and Lara were their best friends, and Lakeside Leisure was what appealed to them, so he and Rudy had been happy to follow. Living below their means meant that they would be able to afford long weekends in Paris or Athens or New Orleans any time they wanted; that was what he looked forward to.

He also knew that even though Helen and Lara were their best friends, he and Rudy were not theirs. Oh yes, they were close, but nothing was closer than two pairs of lesbians. Still, he thought their friendship had a unique advantage. Since men, he felt, bonded with each first and foremost because of sex, and lesbians because of gender, having neither gender nor sex between them meant that their friendship was pure, motivated by none of the chemical or hormonal imperatives or imbalances that made so many relationships destructive and deranged.

And he had been happy to leave New York; it had become a suffocatingly sad place for him. The city he had come out in, first fell in love in, danced nights in till the balls of his feet burned, had the best sex of his life in, had now become a burial ground, a concrete cemetery. Friend upon friend upon friend had died of AIDS, until his phone book had become a history book, until he was no longer sure his past was even real, there were so few friends to corroborate it. Only Rudy.

Through some miracle he felt he did not deserve, both of them remained HIV negative.

So he had been happy to come down here to this place that also had no history, even though its excuse was that it had been built only a dozen years before. It struck him as a frontier, a lush and carelessly beautiful frontier, and he wanted to hide out here with his man for the rest of his days.

And all he wanted Rudy to do was sit still, hold his hand, sigh in time with him. Safe at last. But Rudy wouldn't sit still, and Rich loved him too much to ask.

17

*K*aren had been sitting in her car in the gallery's parking lot for half an hour, with her birdbath painting on the passenger seat next to her. She still hadn't worked up the nerve to go in.

She watched people coming and going, most of whom stayed just a few minutes, surely not enough time to do more than glance around. One couple stayed inside twenty minutes and Karen began to have a dark fantasy that maybe they were buying the hummingbird painting. Next she began to worry that they were robbing the place and had tied Georgia up. She imagined rushing in, surprising them, saving the day, returning Georgia's grateful embrace . . .

She made herself stop. Made herself, because Georgia had been insinuating herself into her daydreams (and a few night dreams) ever since they'd met and had their brief exchange. It was stupid and futile but she didn't seem to have the strength of will to keep it in check. And the worst was, it sickened her to think of hurting Chris, Chris who had saved her from twenty years of marital melancholy. Meeting Chris, seeing her in action, had given Karen the courage to believe life might actually hold some capacity for joy, joy she herself defined. She meant to be loyal to Chris forever, she *wanted* to be loyal to Chris forever — that was why she was down here in a part of the world she would never have moved to otherwise. And yet, she seemed to have caught Georgia Novack like a virus.

Who knew what accounted for it? Maybe her thick cascade of curly chestnut hair. She had imagined how, pulled back with one hand, it would be full, soft and springy in her palm, and how it would expose her throat, a sloping, swan's neck throat, pale and a little over-delicate with age. She had imagined her breasts and large, dark nipples. She had imagined as far as the musky smell of her, the sticky, welcoming taste of her . . .

She shuddered in the starched, air-conditioned air of the car. It was ridiculous and futile. Georgia was straight, married, but for that matter, Karen knew, she herself had been, too. Maybe *that* was it — some need to continue the chain, or rather to break it, to release another woman, to set her free. Or maybe it was none of those things, just flat-footed, blunt-edged vanity, the reliable magnetism of flattery. Yes, Chris was slavishly enthusiastic about her painting, but inside the cocoon of their love and life together, what other response could she be expected to have? Whereas if Georgia thought she had promise, maybe she really did.

Karen sat tensed, tapping without rhythm on the steering wheel, eyes boring into the door of the gallery. She felt the way she did when she was poised at the edge of a difficult intersection, terrified of not making it safely across the racing stream of traffic, but equally terrified of being stuck, inert, unable to get where she needed to go. She felt that way now, unsure how to gauge the risk of proceeding or the disappointment of staying put.

The couple who had been in the gallery so long finally emerged, the man carrying a large, brown-paper wrapped canvas he could barely get his arm around. At least that meant her hummingbird was safe. She took it as a sign. She lifted her own painting off the seat, opened the car door to a furnace-blast of heat, and hurried toward the gallery.

"Oh, hello again," Georgia said, whirling around as Karen's entrance shook the little chimes above the door. "It's Karen, isn't it? Karen bearing gifts?"

Karen felt herself blush, from her throat clear up to her scalp. She felt sure Georgia could sense all the carnal imaginings that had swamped her.

"Not bearing gifts exactly. I'm being bad mannered enough to take you up on your offer to show you some work of mine. It's something I've really just finished — maybe it's not any good at all . . ." She held it out, watching Georgia's face, waiting to seize on the first flicker of reaction.

Georgia frowned at the painting, carried it to hold under a spotlight. She wore a gauzy, floor-length plum dress, light enough that it danced with every breeze and gesture. Georgia studied the painting as Karen studied her. Karen decided in that moment that she wanted to paint Georgia.

"It's . . . lovely, quite lovely," Georgia said. "Very lush but understated. I think I can take it on." She looked up at Karen. "On consignment, of course. You're unknown, your potential's unknown. But let's try, shall we?"

A tremble of joy vibrated in Karen's throat. "Yes, let's try. I'd like that." And she held Georgia's gaze as long as she dared.

18

*R*ich had just stretched out his long, tanned legs on the lounge chair by the pool when the front door bell buzzed. He groaned and considered ignoring it, but then, happily anticipating that maybe it was Helen or Chris or one of the gang, he got up and hurried barefoot back through the freeze-dried air of the house. And freeze-dried was how it felt to him since Rudy kept the air conditioning on perpetually, and at 65 degrees.

"Hello, there — hope I'm not disturbing you," boomed a paunchy, mustached man in gleaming white shirt and shorts. He was reflecting so much sunlight it hurt to look at him. "I'm Bill Seagirt," he said. "Here to see if our new neighbor is a golfer."

"Ah! Hello, Rich Dubrow," Rich said, holding open the door and putting out his hand to shake. He felt himself click into professional mode even though he was wearing only a royal blue Speedo bathing suit. "I'm afraid I'm not a golfer, though. Boating's my sport."

"Not a problem," the man said. "There's time for both now. You live in Florida, you gotta golf. Let me sign you up and me and a bunch of the guys'll give you some pointers. After a couple of weeks, you'll be addicted just like everybody else."

Rich stepped outside to lean against the railing and face Mr. Clean. He towered over the man, so he slouched a bit to seem less intimidating. "That's really neighborly of you — and I don't want to seem unfriendly. But golf's not for me. I have too many memories of doing business on the green to make it seem like recreation now." He shuddered at the memory of the flagrant heterosexuality on display. Sports were invented, after all, so straight men would have something to talk to each other about. "But I'll tell you who are *terrific* golfers. My friends two doors down," Rich said, pointing.

"Oh, yeah?" Bill Seagirt asked. "Who's that?"

"Angie and Ruth Napelstein. Excellent golfers. Give you a run for your money, that's for sure."

"Angie and Ruth — women? So you're a joker, huh?"

Rich folded his arms across his bare chest; he was beginning to feel self-conscious in nothing but his spandex suit. Not because he wasn't in pretty good shape — he was — but because straight men, after all, did not wear Speedo, unless they were twenty-year-old Californians, which clearly this town did not see much of. "No joke," Rich said, trying to smile the way state troopers do when they tell you that yes, you really were doing eighty.

"Yeah, well," Bill Seagirt said, smoothing his mustache with his thumb. "We uh, don't do things that way here. The wives have their card games, we play golf. We don't want the ladies slowing down our game."

"Angie and Ruth would never slow down your game, I promise you that," Rich said. "But I know what you mean. Sometimes women have more in common with women, and men with other men."

Bill Seagirt frowned and pushed his hands into his pockets. Rich knew Bill was at a loss to decide whether or not he was being rebuked. He could see Bill's antenna going, telling him that Rich was not a guy like him. He just didn't know what the hell kind of a guy Rich was instead. "Well uh, you change your mind, you let me know," Bill said. "Everybody knows me at the clubhouse."

"Thanks," Rich said, watching Bill Seagirt go down the walk. "Maybe I'll tell Angie and Ruth to look you up."

Bill raised his hand slightly, without turning around. Rich knew it was not a friendly gesture, and he knew exactly what kind of guy Bill Seagirt was.

19

*F*elicia squeezed Georgia's hand hard in greeting when she reached the table where she was waiting. The two women tried to have lunch together once a month, but today Felicia was especially glad to see her.

She slid into the green cushioned seat across from Georgia, cheered to have a window with a view of the restaurant's backyard garden and duck pond. "How are you, honey? And Hank?" Felicia asked, admiring the way her friend looked in her sleeveless fuchsia sundress; a straw hat was hanging off the side of her chair. Georgia was attractive, but more than that she had style. Felicia was able to admire and enjoy Georgia like a pretty landscape; she did not feel competitive or jealous the way Bunny, for example, did. Maybe it didn't make Felicia a better person. Maybe she was just old enough not to have much vanity left.

The two women exchanged updates, careful to assure the other that everyone's health was fine or at least being successfully managed with a regimen of pills and monitored diet. That was always the first order of business; it was not to be taken for granted at their ages. Georgia explained that the gallery was doing no better and no worse than usual, but that a new woman fresh to Lakeside had brought in a very good painting for Georgia to sell.

It was just the opening Felicia needed. "Oh yes, there's a few new, ah — families that just moved in, in fact, from up north, the New York area. Paxton Court — they've got the whole thing," Felicia said. She waited while the waitress put down their chicken salad platters. "They're all friends actually. I've gotten to know one of them, Helen — she used to be a professional dog trainer, isn't that interesting? I thought at first she said she had a husband — Larry — and we had them over for dinner but it turns out she said *Lara*, and it's a *woman* she lives with, and well, you can imagine our surprise. But they're both *so* lovely, really, though Bunny is threatening all kinds of things already. Can you pass the pepper, Georgia, dear?" Georgia had folded her arms on the starched white tablecloth and was leaning forward, eyeing her a little too keenly, Felicia thought. "The pepper, Georgia?" Felicia prompted.

"Felicia, are you all right? You seem a little wound up."

"Well, I, I just needed to talk about it and I thought you'd understand. You know, given that you and Hank had been city people all your life, though

74

God knows Atlanta is not New York City. Still, it's a darn sight closer than the little bug-blood town in Mississippi where Ted and I spent our whole lives. You know, my daddy was a minister — I don't tell everybody that, it makes some people defensive, I've learned that over the years — and we didn't have a lot of money. My brothers and I did not grow up feeling we were better than other people. We grew up feeling like all of humanity was our brothers and sisters."

Felicia paused to sample her chicken salad and debated whether to say more. Then she looked at Georgia's sympathetic face and got a second wind. "You know, my oldest son — I don't tell everybody down here this, either, not at first, anyway — married a black girl. When he got married, none of our friends came to the wedding. I'd lived there my whole entire adult life, and I sent out a hundred and twenty-five invitations, and not one single person came." Felicia stopped. She didn't want to cry, and she had to concentrate to keep the tears from coming. "It was heart-piercing to me and Ted," she started again. "We love our son and his wife, Cheryl, like one of our own — and oh, how she loves our boy! And you know they had to leave town, of course, after that. Went on their honeymoon and just didn't come back. Moved to Detroit. And our friends didn't come around any more either. Just absolutely heart-piercing. Because you know, when you find the right person to love, well, it just doesn't happen every day and I can't see how people think they've got the right to condemn you for it. I don't see what in hangnail people think it is of their business.

"So you know, naturally I think of my boy when I think of cases like Helen and Lara," Felicia said. "And

I've tried to see why it should matter to people and I just can't. I just *can't*. It's hard for me to be around people like Bunny."

Georgia leaned back in her chair and signaled the waitress. When the smiling young woman came over, Georgia said, "Please bring my friend a gin and tonic."

Felicia gasped as the waitress left on her mission. "Georgia! I don't drink, and certainly not in the middle of the afternoon!"

"Felicia, as your friend, trust me. You can and you will. I've never heard you talk this much in the entire year I've known you, let alone in one sitting. You are what is known as wired, and a drink is the remedy."

"Well, I just don't —"

"*Shhh,*" Georgia said. "That's a terrible story, Felicia, and I couldn't agree with you more. What would gall me is not even having had a chance to tell your so-called friends off."

"I've never been a person to make a scene."

"So, what you're telling me now is that we have lesbians in Lakeside Leisure. Lakeside Lesbians, or Lesbian Lakesiders, so to speak."

Felicia felt her face flush. "Well, yes," she whispered. The "L" word made her a little nervous, and she wished Georgia wouldn't use it. Not out loud anyway.

"I think it's just great. I think we have to protect them from people like Bunny, in the name of your son and his wife. God knows this community needs a little diversity. And I could use some more people around here who support the arts!"

The waitress arrived with the drink and turned away before Felicia could object. "Who was the woman who brought you the painting?"

"Karen Barth," Georgia said.

"Yes, she's one of their group. I met her briefly. She was younger. A little guarded, I thought."

"That's right," Georgia said, gazing out the window, rubbing her temple slowly. "Shy. Like maybe she hasn't quite come into her own yet."

Felicia picked up the drink and took a gulp. She waited to see if it had any immediate effect. The idea of getting drunk had begun to appeal to her.

"Easy, there, Felicia — that isn't iced tea." Georgia speared a piece of chicken. "You know, Felicia, I love Hank. But sometimes I wonder what on God's earth we have in common. His interest in art stops at the price tag. His idea of the perfect weekend is pulling some weeds and hitting some golf balls. The last romantic thing he did was in nineteen fifty-two when he asked me to marry him in a hot air balloon and then got so sick from his fear of heights that he threw up the dinner we'd just had together over the side of the basket."

Felicia laughed so hard she slapped the table and sent her fork catapulting to the table in front of them with a crash of silverware. Fortunately, no one was sitting there. She had another gulp of her drink.

"All I mean is," Georgia said, "I'd never argue with anyone that men are all they're cracked up to be. But we don't have any choice about loving them, do we? And I imagine lesbians feel the same way about women, too."

When it was time to leave, Felicia could see that Georgia had decided she was too drunk to drive, but Felicia knew she wasn't. She was merely merry with good will. She got on her golf cart and headed home, as Georgia followed along protectively in her car. She was bone-deep grateful to Georgia for the chat; she felt surrounded by love and affection on all fronts. And when she parked the cart under the car port and waved to Georgia, she headed into the house, calling out lustily for Ted, who was as yet unaware that it was about to be his lucky day.

20

*A*fter dinner, which all four women helped prepare, they moved outside to sit on the lounge chairs arranged around the pool. It was one of those facts of lesbian life that Lara stopped to think about only occasionally: that everyone pitched in. She was usually reminded at a straight party, when, during cleanup, the men seemed to magically scatter without reproach, while any woman who didn't collect in the kitchen, sleeves rolled up, was condemned as lazy and rude.

Lara had speared citronella torches strategically along the rim of the pool; it reminded her of the tropical-themed Florida hotels she had stayed in as a child on family vacations when both Florida and vacations themselves seemed exotic. The memory warmed and saddened her. She had never gotten around to telling her parents the truth about her life with Helen, and the older they had gotten, the more impossible it seemed. Whenever she thought of it now, it ate away at her that when it came to knowing how they might have reacted, her imagination would be all she'd ever have.

Chris carried out two last glasses of wine and handed one to Lara; Helen and Karen had declined, protesting that they'd had too much. "It's up to us, as usual," Chris said happily. The sky was two broad swaths of dark blue, but wasn't yet night; there was just a hint of stars, ready in their places. The torches roared like giant match sticks, the breeze occasionally sending a coil of heat and smoky-sweet perfume in the women's direction. They scraped the lounge chairs around on the concrete till they'd made a crescent.

"Next time we do this, let's hire Rudy's catering," Helen said, laughing.

"How's he doing with that?" Karen asked.

"Really well," Helen said. "Too well for Rich's taste. He says it's like Rudy never retired."

"Except that, of course, Rich has, so now there's an imbalance," Lara said.

"So what's with Rudy?" Chris asked. "Why's he knocking himself out?"

"He says he just needs to get it off the ground," Helen said. "Then he says he'll kick back, let the cooks he's trained run the show, and watch the money roll in."

"Sounds reasonable. Will he do it?" Karen asked.

"That's what Rich is waiting to see," Lara said.

"A cautionary tale," Chris said, grabbing Karen's

hand. "You were supposed to be painting just for yourself, but ever since you brought that first one to be sold, you've been driving yourself like a one-woman assembly line."

"Oh, you're exaggerating," Karen said, tugging her hand free.

Lara noted the move with discomfort. She glanced at Chris and saw from her face that she was stung.

Lara put her head back, letting the conversation swirl around her. She had to smother her protective impulses when it came to Chris, had to remind herself that it wasn't possible for four people to maintain a friendship if she was always ready to criticize one-fourth of it. After three years, it was Chris's place alone to make clear to Karen how she wanted to be treated in their relationship.

Lara concentrated instead on the feeling of the heat seeping out of the plastic chair, the arm rests growing cool and slippery under her bare arms. The sky was now uniformly black, without a moon and only a few stars to illuminate it. With her left hand she held her wine glass, and with her right she reached over and laced her fingers through Helen's, who squeezed back with a lover's promise.

". . . so the day after my letter arrived by registered mail," Chris was saying, "Angie and Ruth got a call from a clubhouse manager, saying that of course they were entitled to the household discount and they were sorry about the misunderstanding."

"No kidding. Good for them, then, for making a fuss," Helen said. "I have to admit, Angie and Ruth sometimes use a battering ram when a toothpick would do the job, but their hearts are always in the right place."

"Yeah, but now they have to live with the consequences," Chris said.

"What do you mean?" Karen asked.

"I mean that now they have to go to the clubhouse and see how they're treated," Chris said. "Admittance doesn't always mean acceptance, especially when people's hands have been forced."

"I'm surprised to hear that coming from you," Karen said.

"It doesn't mean I don't think they shouldn't have done what they did," Chris said. "I just mean that I saw this over and over again my whole career. People make the mistake of thinking that a courtroom victory means that everybody agrees to play fair from that day forward. Sure it means some principle was acknowledged, but it can't change people's hearts and minds. And it's those hearts and minds that keep operating once the courtroom is cleared."

"Pretty depressing," Karen said.

"Well, classic example," Chris said. "The men in your ex-husband's case won a moral point — and they got some cash to boot. But it didn't wipe out prejudice against blacks."

"Right," said Lara. "That's what dinner parties are for. Did you tell everyone about our night with Ted and Felicia, honey?"

Helen proceeded to relate the story of the dinner invitation, complete with Lara's mistaken identity. Chris and Karen laughed and cheered their way through it.

"Is she the sweet little old lady who came around with the cups of sugar?" Karen asked.

"Yes, that's her," Helen said.

"Be careful who you call a sweet little old lady," Chris said. "We're all on the brink of qualifying."

"Old is inevitable. Sweet is not," Karen said.

"Thank God," Lara said. "How else would we tell each other apart?"

They stayed outside and gossiped till they all complained of a slight chill. Helen and Lara walked Chris and Karen to the front door and kissed them goodnight, watching as they headed down the walk to their own house.

Lara kissed Helen's sleeveless shoulder, fragrant with the last traces of her perfume mixed with the smoke of their cooking and candles. "Did you feel like Karen was a little irritable with Chris tonight?" Lara asked.

"Oh, I don't know," Helen said, turning to put her arms around Lara's waist and rest her cheek on her collar bone. "Maybe, now that you mention it. But nothing I wouldn't chalk up to a little menopause."

"Mmmm, maybe," Lara said. "Maybe that's all it was." And they headed up to bed.

21

*B*unny prided herself on being driven and effective, and she congratulated herself on her success as she headed to Helen and Lara's house.

Lakeside Leisure consisted of two hundred households, and she had collected the signatures of owners of one hundred and fifty-two of them who had listened to her lament: that four new houses had been bought and painted ostentatious shades of purple and lavender. Not only were these colors that did not compliment the rest of the community, Bunny had reasoned, but it turned out that the colors were politically symbolic of gay activism! The owners ought to be made to get in line. All that she was asking was that they change the colors of their houses to something that fit in better, like egg shell or cream or even pale pink, if they must.

Most people whose doorbell she had rung hadn't needed much coaxing. Purple houses made them scared and suspicious and smacked of shanty neighborhoods and loud and crass behavior. And then, just as she had planned it, their eyes narrowed in anger at the explanation of why such colors had been chosen in the first place: gay propagandizing. She was no bigot, Bunny was quick to explain. This was America and no one was saying these gays didn't have a right to breathe. It was just that, aside from the colors being awful, no one should have the right to make a political statement with their siding if it was going to offend the rest of the community. A few people had asked if there was anything they could do to throw them out wholesale, but Bunny knew enough to discourage this. Besides, she hinted darkly, such drastic measures might not be necessary if these radicals came to understand that their values were not welcome here.

She had a few rude surprises at the forty-eight holdout houses. She had known not to ask Felicia and Georgia and a few others she knew to have arty and liberal leanings. And when a handful of black owners came to the door, she had slunk away, pretending to have rung the wrong doorbell; she couldn't imagine their taking kindly to any conversation about "types who didn't fit in." But she didn't count on being cursed down the driveway by a number of others. "What's next?" screamed one red-faced man. "Regulations about the kinds of shrubs and what colors the cars parked in front of our houses should be?" He hadn't paid a hundred thou for his house, he had raged on nastily, to have some old biddy dictate to him about how to hang his toilet paper. She had run in frantic little steps to get away from him. To her shock, a couple of others had called her a fascist and slammed the door on her nose, and the rest had looked bored or fearful or uncomprehending, and said they simply didn't want to get into any ruckus about anything.

But here she was, at the end of a three-week effort, with a majority of signatures from the community, demanding that the Paxton Court Perverts, as she had come to think of them, repaint their propaganda houses. She considered it a victory for decency. And now she was at Helen and Lara's door, ringing the bell, and she would explain exactly that.

Helen answered the door and, as Felicia had described, the dog was right at her ankle. "Good morning," Helen said.

"Good morning. I'm Bunny Seagirt. I know who you are but I don't believe we've met," she said.

"Come in, won't you?" Helen said.

"No, I don't think so," Bunny said. "I've only come to deliver this," she said, handing over the signed petition.

The dog started growling, a low, rumbly, sinister sound.

"Emma, quiet," Helen said, in a sharp tone that silenced the dog. "Please forgive me. She never does that. She must have . . . something must have frightened her. Are you sure you won't come in?"

"No, no. I'm very sorry to say this isn't exactly a social visit." She saw Helen's expression grow grave. "I mean, of course, I'm hoping everything can be resolved peacefully, but I think you'll want to read what's inside your envelope first. Good day," Bunny said, and turned, starting down the path for the sidewalk. And if it wasn't her imagination, she could swear she heard that menacing mutt start growling again.

22

*T*hey had fought.

It had been one of the ugliest fights between them in Rich's recent memory. Here they were, a Saturday night of their retirement, and Rudy had to work, thanks to a fiftieth wedding anniversary celebration, sixty people in attendance, and a request for Rudy's most complicated menu. This was just the kind of bullshit their retiring together was supposed to eliminate, Rich had screamed. Rudy had promised, Rich charged, that this was going to be a sideline, a little part-time distraction, but it was fucking taking over their lives. Rudy was congenitally incapable of doing anything half-way; Rich should have known not to let him start this. Rudy had raged back that Rich was being a controlling bitch as usual, that obviously there was no way to get out of this now, and why couldn't he just be a little patient and let him get the fucking thing off the ground? Because, Rich had boomed, you never know when to stop. Once it was established as a nice little catering place, there would be another level to conquer — then another and another. If he had wanted to work his butt off, Rich accused, why had they moved down to this armpit of a place? They could have stayed in Manhattan and made real money. In the end, Rudy had stormed out, saying he was fucking late enough as it was, and Rich had screamed after him not to expect him to be waiting fireside when he got back.

And he wouldn't be, because Rich was now three hours north in the bar they had scoped out when they'd first moved here, and he had already booked himself a room at the nearby motel. His plan was to go back and sleep there alone, but he wasn't ruling out company.

The place was the kind he remembered from his suburban New Jersey youth — an innocuous-looking building plopped down in the middle of a parking lot at the end of some deserted road. As a result, the bar was fairly large, but drab and unremarkable, with no imagination or ambition. There were a few scattered pinball machines, a dartboard, a huge bar where he had attached himself, and a dance floor above which hung one of those mirrored balls he thought had been banned to the Smithsonian after 1979. The music was old disco and a little new techno pop, all deafening.

It was crowded. The air conditioning was barely keeping the place comfortable. More than a few men were already shirtless, their chests streaked with sweat after dancing for an hour at a stretch. The place claimed to be mixed — there were a few lesbians huddled together like frightened love birds, suspicious of his attempts to draw them into conversation — but mainly the territory was male. A few guys had cruised him, but no one interesting, or at least not that he had noticed, still rewinding in his head the fight with Rudy, still turning over all their arguments, trying to figure out the real source of tension. He knew Rudy was terrified of being bored or idle, but it wasn't fair of him to work out those demons at the expense of their joint happiness.

"Looks like you could use a fresh one," said a low, caramelly voice at his shoulder. Rich angled himself to see who was confidently gesturing over the harried bartender, ordering two of whatever it was that Rich was drinking. What struck Rich first was how young the man was: twenty, twenty-one, maybe still in college if he was being leisurely about it. And that he was beautiful. Short, thick, blue-black hair, a strong, serious face, somehow old-fashioned, the kind that used to work so well on Marine recruiting posters. He nearly matched Rich in height, but this boy was built, carefully so, the kind of sculpted muscle that came from lifting, not manual labor. He wore a tank top, a ribbon of sweat staining the front, and black jeans with ankle boots. This was a boy who could have anyone in this bar, and any bar like it in the state, Rich knew. What, Rich wondered, did he want with an old man like him?

"I'm Greg," the young man said, holding out his hand for the kind of shake given in boardrooms, not barrooms. "You're not from around here — I can tell by the accent," Greg said.

"And you're not either," Rich said. "I can tell by the attitude."

The boy smiled slowly, at first for effect, but then it

turned genuine. "Let's dance," he said, catching Rich's hand firmly and leading him to the floor before Rich had a chance to stall.

They shoved onto the floor in between sweating, jumping men, the music pounding like boxing gloves against Rich's ears. It was so loud the melody was flattened to a thumping of bass. Greg seemed lost to it immediately, his eyes shut, his head thrown back, his hands clawing for the ceiling, hopping on his toes. Rich struggled to find his step, too trapped inside his head to really let go. But watching this boy could persuade him. He pushed the image of Rudy and their fight out of his mind, tried to time-travel back to his youth, to pretend this was a night lost in space, somewhere back when he and New York and all his friends were young and healthy and unsuspecting.

He felt his hips come alive, felt his shoulders loosen and move. Greg was gone, he realized, in a small spasm of disappointment and shame. Then he sensed Greg behind him. Yes, that was him, Greg's hands on his hips, on his thighs, his groin feinting against Rich's butt. Rich felt his whole body blush with pleasure, a coiling tightness start in his groin. The music pounded on but now he liked it, was inside its howling, screaming onslaught, and the bodies around him were reduced to scent and movement and heat. Greg was somewhere and everywhere behind him and in front of him, and Rich was so hard inside his jeans it was impossible and ridiculous. He grabbed Greg's wrist hard and yanked him through the crowd, squeezing along backs and butts till they landed in the humid freedom along the bar.

"Had enough already?" Greg asked when they both got their breath.

"No, actually," Rich said, making up his mind on the spot. "I have a place nearby. Interested?" The animated expression on Greg's face sagged. "Did I say the wrong thing? I thought —"

"No, no, it's not you. It's just that you hear a lot of horror stories. You know," Greg said.

"Ah, that's true. Except that the risk is usually the other way around. The older man, flattered into recklessness by the attentions of the handsome young — unbeknownst to him — straight homophobic psychokiller, is the one who ends up criss-crossed with the phone wire, robbed and left for dead."

"Do you always have such inviting pick-up lines?" Greg asked, his smile unsteady.

"I'm sorry," Rich said, seeing that the boy really was rattled, not truly as slick as his lines. That's when Rich decided his gut was right: he had nothing to fear from this boy. Maybe there was a wife, or at least a girlfriend, who lived nearby. It happened all the time. And that would be just fine with Rich; after all, he was married, too. "Look, I'm safe," Rich said, pulling his wallet out of his back pocket and opening it to his driver's license. "That's who I am. Have a good look at the address."

Greg studied the license. "I know the area. Seems a bit tame for you."

"Well, it is. That's why I'm here tonight."

They each took their own cars back to the motel. Fortunately, no one was at the front desk when they walked through the tiny lobby; Rich wouldn't have relished the picture he made, a well dressed, silver-haired man bringing a handsome, T-shirted boy a third his age back to his one-night rental.

Rich had barely turned around from closing the

door when Greg cupped the light switch. "Don't turn it on," he said. He unbuckled Rich's khakis and, leaving Rich pressed against the door with his pants at his ankles, he crouched and took him in his mouth. For a few moments, out of habit, Rich tried to take in the details of the unfamiliar room, the way he had countless other times, finding himself in the apartments of men he barely knew, trying to orient himself quickly in case . . . in case of what, he scarcely knew. In case the police or a landlord or an angry, homicidal lover charged in — so he would always know the quickest exit or hiding place.

But soon the top of his head was lifting off and all he could focus on was Greg's warm mouth, and he came with a grizzly-bear groan of release.

Greg pushed himself up with his palms, flushed and smiling. "Sorry to jump you like that," he whispered.

"Did you hear any complaints?" Rich said, stepping out of his pants and shedding his shirt, too, as he led Greg over to the bed. He threw back the bedspread and sheets in one impatient fling, and he could feel Greg's growing nervousness. He was worried the boy was going to bolt before he even got to see him naked, let alone touch him.

"I'm not sure about this," Greg said sitting on the edge of the bed, suddenly passive, letting Rich pull the damp tank top over his head, letting him yank off his boots and jeans. His hard-on in his gleaming white briefs was huge, and Rich found himself erect again.

"Don't worry, I've got condoms," Rich said, pushing him down and turning him over. His back and buttocks were as smooth, muscled, and innocent-looking as the boys Rich remembered from his college locker-room days.

"No, I can't do this," Greg said, whirling around, pushing away.

"Hey, it's okay, it's fine," Rich said, falling back on his heels. "We'll do whatever you like."

Greg hugged his knees to his chest; Rich had trouble keeping his eyes off the enormous erection straining against Greg's underwear, and it didn't make him feel much like chatting.

"I don't know what I like," Greg whispered. "I've never done . . . *this* before. I mean, with someone I don't know."

"Ah, I see," Rich said, understanding all at once why Greg picked him tonight, above all the other hard-bodied young things. "That's just fine. We can find out. I'll show you what I know." He reached tentatively for the waistband of Greg's underwear and tugged slowly, making Greg meet his eyes till he felt the boy trusted him.

For the next hour, they wrestled and ranged around the bed. Greg had instincts nearly better than experience, Rich discovered, and he forced himself to focus on his cock, not the stirrings of his heart, which was warming to the boy's sweet, careful caresses, and the soft, hungry kisses he allowed only after he'd come three times. Finally, tangled in the gummy sheets, they stopped by unspoken agreement, flat on their backs, spent.

"I have to get going," Greg said, rubbing circles on Rich's chest with his palm.

Rich roused himself from the brink of sleep, pulling himself up onto his elbows. Home to that wife or fiancée, Rich figured, or maybe even parents. It wasn't out of the question that Greg might still live at home, in that period after college when more and more young people had no idea how to start their adult lives. Rich realized he didn't know a single tangible thing about this boy: not his occupation or hometown or alma mater or even last name. He knew a fair amount of other arguably more important things about him, none of which would ever help him find him again. But that was as it should be, Rich scolded himself. And no doubt how Greg wanted it. Why else would he be leaving?

Greg dressed in silence; Rich watched admiringly the body he had just traversed so intimately. How had the tables gotten so turned? he wondered in the gathering sadness. Just a few nights of sleep ago he himself was the young, beautiful man, dashing out doors, another adventure just ahead of him. And even though he had no respectable complaints — his life had been successful, in love and in work; he had lost so many friends to AIDS, and yet he and Rudy had been spared — he felt cheated somehow. His work, though so often despised, had still defined him. Neither he nor Rudy, he realized, had any idea how to have a relationship full-time. And now that they had the chance to learn, they were too old, too stubborn, maybe too afraid to get that much more attached just at the moment when their age seemed to dictate that they must shortly be parted.

"You're not angry with me, are you?" Greg said.

Rich started; he had nearly forgotten Greg was still in the room. "God no," he said, smiling broadly at seeing Greg transformed, through his clothes, back into the Marine with attitude. "Why would I be angry? Tonight was terrific."

"And you're not interested in more than just tonight, right?"

It wasn't lost on Rich that Greg's tone was a touch petulant. This wasn't the voice of agreement, it was a submerged accusation. "Well, it was as far as I'd planned."

"Yeah, me too," Greg said, quickly. "Well, maybe I'll see you around then." He stuffed his hands in his front pockets and shrugged. At the door, he hung his head for a moment. "I, uh — maybe this sounds dumb, but uh, I want to say thanks. You know."

"Yes, I do know," Rich said. He knew that and a lot more, but he kept it to himself as Greg closed the door behind him.

23

*M*y God, it's decorating discrimination!" Angie exclaimed, reading Bunny Seagirt's petition. Helen had rounded up everybody she could. There was no answer at the guys', and Angie had come alone because Ruth was sleeping late.

"Look, if you have another lawyer letter in mind, forget it," Chris said.

"I think Bunny and her purple posse know this isn't a legal matter," Helen said.

"See, exactly my point from the other night," Chris said, addressing Karen.

"We should fight fire with fire," Lara said. "Send them back our own petition saying we find *beige* offensive."

"But we'd be hopelessly outnumbered, that's clear," Helen said.

"Something more aggressive is called for," Angie said. "I say, in the dead of night, we paint *everyone's* house purple. Then ours won't stand out, we can tell her."

"I say we just ignore it," Karen said. "It's too stupid to even dignify."

The group, assembled around the white wrought iron breakfast table in the screened-in patio, fell silent to consider Karen's suggestion. "We'd have to be prepared to say something, though, when Bunny comes back to confront us about why we haven't repainted the houses," Helen said.

"We could just say we appreciate the input but we pass on the opportunity to conform," Chris said.

"That's classy," Lara said, smiling at her friend.

"Ack — it's cowardly," Angie said.

"Jesus, I didn't come down here to fight everyone every day," Karen said.

"Neither did I," Angie shot back. "If *they'd* stop violating our rights I could go read classics by the pool all day, the way I want."

"Okay, ladies, let's settle down," Helen said. "We definitely didn't come here to fight with each other."

"Angie, what do you say we just ignore it for now?" Lara said. "Then, if Bunny continues to be obnoxious, we can consider something else."

The early morning sun glinted off the pool while everyone waited for Angie's answer. "All right," she said, drawing out the word in childish protest. "But if I were you, I'd be thinking over that 'something else' pretty seriously."

24

*C*heers!" Georgia said, clicking her champagne glass against Karen's. She had sold Karen's birdbath painting for three hundred and fifty dollars, of which Georgia got thirty percent — and she had rushed out to get a bottle of champagne and called Karen to come to the gallery to celebrate. It was a more extravagant gesture than she usually made, but she felt Karen needed the encouragement. And given Felicia's news, Georgia wanted Karen to know that she had a friend in her, just in case people like Bunny Seagirt were determined to make it appear that everyone in Lakeside Leisure was a swampland bigot. She thought tonight might present a way to bring that up, too.

"Cheers, and thank you, Georgia, for your help," Karen said.

"So when do I get the next one?" Georgia asked, swiveling happily in her favorite red tufted chair behind her desk in the gallery's paneled office.

"Well, I am actually working on something. Another backyard scene."

"Excellent. I think that's the way to go," Georgia said. "For now, stick with what you know works. And besides, the way business goes down here, five neighbors of the woman who bought your painting will come marching in, asking if I have another one just like it."

Karen laughed. "If we're both lucky. But actually, I had another idea, too. Something that we wouldn't necessarily sell, but something I'd find personally rewarding because I want practice in portraits, and something I could give you as a real thank you."

"That's not necessary — don't lose sight of the fact that I'm profiting here, too, Karen."

"I just want to, though. I'd like to do your portrait."

Georgia registered a quiver of both resistance and delight. No one had ever asked to do her portrait before. On the other hand, she wasn't sure she was comfortable submitting to the kind of scrutiny being a model required. "That's flattering, Karen, but you know, with my life and temperament, I really wouldn't be able to sit still long enough for you."

"Well, maybe you could keep it in mind — if anything changes," Karen said hurriedly, and Georgia saw that the turndown had rattled her.

"Anyway, how are you liking Lakeside? Is it starting to feel anything like home yet?"

"Home? Well, that's an interesting comparison," Karen said, putting her champagne glass down and fluffing the paisley pillows next to her on the couch. "Because it assumes home is a desirable thing, and all my life that wasn't true."

"Oh, I'm sorry," Georgia said. Now it was her turn to be taken aback; she hadn't meant to solicit something quite so raw and sad.

"I don't mean my childhood home. That was fine, I suppose, though we weren't an especially close family. We were well off, I was an only child. I married a rich man I thought I'd grow to love a bit more than I did — but I didn't. We had two sons. One lives in Texas, the other in California. I see them twice a year. They're both closer to their father. They blame me for the divorce."

"And who do you blame?" Georgia asked.

Karen stretched out on the couch, her head on the pillows. "This is a little too close to a therapy setting, isn't it? Me on the couch, you over there behind the desk. Now *that* makes me feel at home."

"Oh, no. The champagne makes all the difference." Both women laughed. "But you're happy now?" Georgia asked.

"Happier than I've ever been," Karen said.

Georgia hesitated, but then decided it was best to dive in quickly. "I think it's a very civilized thing to do — fall in love with another woman. Believe me, plenty of days with our husbands, a lot of us heteros wish we could."

Karen turned her head slowly. "So you know then? How?"

"You've never lived in a small town, have you? That's what these little villages are, you know. You should get used to that."

Karen turned away again and stared up at the ceiling. "I know you mean well, but there was nothing civilized about it. I thought I was losing my mind. My husband threatened to run me out of town for humiliating him, and would have, if he hadn't had enough problems of his own with a lawsuit that ultimately bankrupted him. My sons treat me like I'm an alien. And for a long time I *felt* like an alien. You try joining a completely different culture at fifty years old, where nearly everyone else has known the customs and language for thirty years, and they're more interested in catching you in a mistake than showing you the ropes."

"I'm sorry," Georgia said, feeling more ashamed at her ignorance than her words could convey. She sat chastened in her chair, and stopped swiveling.

"It's sort of a ridiculous position to be in," Karen continued. "I have nearly nothing in common with the person I'm closest to. We've lived our entire adult lives in —" Karen put her fingertips to her temple and shook her head — "*drastically* different worlds. I was the society wife of a rich man raising two sons to be worthy of the power they were going to inherit. She was an ACLU lawyer and a lesbian from in utero, if you believe her version, who spent her life among women and underdogs. But I fell in love — with her strength, her moral purpose, her sweetness, her attentiveness, her devotion. All the things I had always wanted from my husband." Karen looked over again and smiled wryly. "Pretty funny, huh?"

"Funny, no, of course not," Georgia said. She felt like she was walking on ice now, and she was uncomfortable not to have her usual sure-footedness. She had always thought of herself as sophisticated, advanced even, simply for not being a hate-mongering homophobe — see, she congratulated herself, she even knew the lingo. Being in the art world her whole life, she had known her share of gay men and lesbians. Or thought she'd known them. But now she felt conspicuously ignorant of all the subtleties and shadings. She hadn't ever really gotten to know how they lived their lives, what sacrifices were made. She'd just learned the jokes and a few of the cues — and she even thought she understood what was erotic about men and men, and women and women together. But now she was getting a hint that maybe that was knowing not much at all.

"Well, I find I have come to think a lot of it is funny," Karen said, although nothing about her tone was lighthearted or comic.

"But I have to ask you, Karen — stop me if I'm being offensive — do you think you were always a lesbian and didn't know it? Or is there such a thing as, as . . . I don't know . . . serial sexuality or something like that?"

Karen laughed. "Serial sexuality, I like that. I don't know. When I look back, I think of a friendship I had in college with one of my sorority sisters and I think now that maybe I was in love with her. But I had absolutely no context in which to recognize it, let alone act on it. Thank God, too, because I probably would have had a nervous breakdown. But did I not love my husband because I should have had a wife all those years? I can't say. My husband wasn't very lovable as a *person,* I see that now."

"Do you think you'd ever be with a man again?" Georgia asked.

"Theoretically, I suppose. But I find now that — loving Chris aside — my attractions, crushes, whatever, have been only on other women." She sat up then, fluffing her pillow-flattened hair. "So," Karen said with finality, downing what was left of her champagne.

"You're not going already?" Georgia asked, disappointed that their interesting conversation was ending with so much left unresolved and unrevealed.

"Oh, I have to. Chris will be waiting," Karen said, going to the door. "And won't Hank be waiting for you?" Her smile was . . . Georgia thought the right word was *sympathetic.*

25

*H*elen threw the red rubber ball high and far, watching it shrink to a pin dot against the cloudless sky. Emma ran backwards, her snout skyward, trying to gauge the best position for capture. Then she leapt, her white and brown coat flying in all directions like a wave breaking, and clamped her teeth down firmly. Swishing her tail in dog delight, she bounded back over, dropping the wet ball in the grass at Helen's feet.

"Good girl," Helen congratulated, patting Emma's side firmly. They had played a game of catch nearly every day for Emma's six years of life, and the dog never tired of it. Even so, Helen praised her for every retrieval; she suspected Emma was as addicted to that as the running and leaping. It was important in all things in life, Helen thought, never to take pleasures for granted, never to stop showing gratitude. Love was not the least of these things.

In fact, Helen considered, calling Emma to her side to stroll farther into the park, if there was any secret to her and Lara's longevity — and she called it secret only because that was how people inevitably put it to them when they asked, as if she and Lara were willfully hiding something — it was that: not taking each other for granted. Why was it that so many couples practiced and honed bad habits — griping and whining and bickering — but found it easy to abandon all the niceties of courting, the deference and politeness, the eagerness to compliment and please? She and Lara both seemed to have the instinct to guard and preserve those small, loving rituals and as a result, Helen believed, they never stopped feeling them. She still, after more than three decades, registered a dip of disappointment if she came home and didn't find Lara there, or felt a tug of regret if Lara had to go away without her. She still felt a little trill of joy opening her eyes in the morning, finding Lara there, being able to press herself to the warmth of her back, sneaking her head onto Lara's pillow, watching Lara's first tentative smile of the day as she woke and turned to look at her.

Helen walked with Emma slowly through the park, under the swimming-pool blue sky, Emma occasionally stopping to take a noisy inhale of a patch of grass. Her and Lara's life together had been as happy as any, Helen mulled, maybe happier. They had both had that rare thing of loving their work, though Lara insisted on occasionally making herself miserable because she wasn't saving a Third World country or helping to find a cure for AIDS. Not that those weren't worthwhile, even imperative things to do, but it wasn't always possible to do them at one's own particular job, and Helen had sometimes longed for Lara to more often relax and just enjoy the good fortune of being a truly great and skilled lawyer. As far as Helen was concerned for herself, she'd have paid someone to let her do the job she had, so to have people pay *her* was nearly unbelievable. Not that she let that stop her from being a tough negotiator with her contracts; she knew what she was worth. She worked so much and so closely with the dogs she handled all her life that she was certain she could have picked them out blindfolded from a roomful of other specimens of the breed. Sometimes at night she'd dream only of their textures: a peach-fuzz belly, a slippery nose, the diamond-hard whiteness of a tooth.

Beyond that, she and Lara had always been each other's real life. They had always come together at the end of the day — or the week if Lara had been traveling — knowing that the other was the warm hearth of their lives. They never secretly felt relieved to be away from the other — Helen felt this anyway, and was willing to gamble it was true for Lara. Her life before Lara had not been unremarkable but it was uninteresting to her now, unmarked, as it was, by this great love. She let her mind wander briefly to Bunny Seagirt and the workings of her foul, twisted heart, but only to vow not to let her ruin her day, let alone the rest of her life, in this place where they were all going to grow old together.

"Hey, girl," Helen said, flopping one of Emma's ears. The dog turned to look up at her, her mahogany eyes squinted in happiness. Then she jogged a few paces ahead, checking over her shoulder, as if to say, Helen thought, look at all that waits ahead for us, we don't have a minute to waste.

26

*A*ngie was at the deep end of the clubhouse's indoor pool, her elbows supporting her weight at the edge, her torso stretched out wavily in front of her, her toes breaking the water's surface, pink bulbs at the end of white feet. Ruth had promised to join her for laps as soon as she had finished on the treadmill.

Angie had just started her underwater bicycle exercise when she spotted him, the man who had stalked her in the supermarket that day. He was headed over from the other side of the pool, a long white towel draped around his neck that didn't successfully cover the gray-furred paunch above his red, white and blue trunks. She thought to swim away—some days even she didn't relish a confrontation — but then the memory of his arrogance made her angry enough to hold her ground.

He stopped behind her and knelt down on the ceramic tile, one elbow resting on his knee. "I don't believe you ever gave me your name when we had the pleasure of meeting in the supermarket," he said, his salt-and-pepper mustache stretching up his face in a thin line. "I'm Bill, in case you forgot." He held out his hand for a shake.

Angie turned her head just the slightest bit and ignored his hand. She looked him over slowly, hoping to make him break out into a self-conscious sweat. "Why don't you just call me 'old dyke,' the way you did that day?"

His cheeks and nose went crimson, and his lips parted a little in what she guessed was a suppressed gasp. "Look, that was ill-mannered of me, but you drew your sword first, it seems to me. If anyone's going to hold a grudge, it ought to be me. And seeing how I'm not, I'd think you'd have the decency not to, too."

"Well, you misjudge my decency." There was no point, Angie saw, in debating with him the predatory heterosexism of his come-on, so she decided it might be easier if she could get him to write her off as a hopeless crank.

"I've offended you," he said. "Let me make it up to you. Let me take you to dinner at La Mare," he said, leaning in to breathe the name into her ear. "It's the best restaurant you'll find for three hundred miles. They're known for their —"

"Are you married?" Her underwater pedaling got a notch more furious.

"Well, yes, but I'm not suggesting —"

"Well, *I'm* suggesting. I don't cheat on my partner,

but if I were so inclined, I'd do it with your wife, not you."

He pulled back, clutching his towel, and tittered nervously. "You're a real joker, huh?"

Just at that moment, Angie felt someone standing behind them, and turned to see Ruth, dabbing at her flushed face with a striped towel. She could tell Ruth was trying to read their expressions to figure out if this was trouble. "This is another old dyke I'd like you to meet. My old dyke, specifically. Dr. Ruth Naplestein. She's a gynecologist, so be sure to let your wife know if she's changing doctors."

"Actually, I'm not practicing anymore," Ruth said, holding out her hand, "but I'd be happy to give her a recommendation."

"I don't see what I've done to deserve to be mocked," Bill said, struggling creakily to his feet. The tile was cold and slick, Angie knew, and as he rose, he began to tilt. A little whimper broke free from his lips as he plunged sidelong into turquoise water with an enormous splash.

Angie shot Ruth a triumphant smile as she watched Bill's flabby body sink, his white towel spiraling down after him like a deep-sea plant. "The masher from the supermarket," Angie explained to Ruth, who was eyeing the bottom of the pool with concern, Angie noted. Slowly, slowly, he surfaced, his head bobbing above the surface with a spray of water and his startled cry, "Help! I can't swim." He immediately sank again.

"Shit," Ruth said, tossing aside her towel and diving gracefully into the pool. When Angie realized he wasn't clowning, she dove under the surface and joined Ruth, grabbing onto Bill's slippery, blubbery body and hauling him to the surface.

"*Ack! Awk!* " he wheezed when they had his head above water, one of his dead-weight arms pressing down over a shoulder of each woman. They swam with him to the shallow end, where they were able to deposit him on his butt on the steps. A small cluster of people had gathered, to murmur questions and concerns, but he waved off any need of an ambulance.

"But I'll tell you," he said, his words coming slowly between deep, noisy breaths, "what I do need. I need a cop. To press charges. Against these two. This one," he said, puffing and pointing at Angie, "propositions my wife — my *wife!* — and then this other one, knowing I can't swim, shoves me into the deep end."

Angie felt herself start to shake, partly from the sheer physical exertion of hauling this man's ungrateful ass the length of the pool, and partly from the rage that was bubbling up from her toes. She lunged for him, but Ruth grabbed her from behind and gripped her tightly around the waist.

"Get ahold of yourself," Ruth reprimanded in a harsh whisper.

Angie scanned the startled, fleshy old faces blinking at them from poolside. "He's a liar and a coward," she shouted up at them.

"Come on, Angie," Ruth said, tugging on her hand. "Let's not start a riot."

And uncharacteristically, Angie let herself be led quietly from the pool. The biggest workout she was going to get from this clubhouse, she saw, was just fighting to be allowed to come in peace.

27

*A*lthough he had gone to bed at two a.m., Rudy was wide awake by seven. He lay in bed, his hands behind his head, looking out the window at the morning sunshine bathing their backyard orange tree.

He had known Rich wouldn't be home when he got in. Rich did not make idle threats. There was a chance, Rudy knew, that he was no farther than this block, crashing at Lara and Helen's. But more likely he had headed for that bar they had found together. Rudy had just been too tired to check the garage for Rich's car before he went to bed. But he was willing to bet Rich drank till his anger numbed, then crawled off to a motel's too soft, too narrow bed. If he was getting up now, he probably felt like shit, with a hangover and a backache, and it served him right. Rudy didn't imagine that Rich would have actually picked someone up; his mood had been too pissy and he was in general too finicky. The chances of some local being tempting enough to overcome all that were remote.

It wasn't that it would have shocked him if Rich had; all through their twenty years together, there'd been occasional other men, most lasting not more than a few weeks and being introduced later to the other simply as a new friend. But since AIDS, they did that less and less, and frankly, that was fine with Rudy. He'd lost interest in the game years before, mainly because he'd finally satisfied himself that there wasn't some grand undiscovered experience — physical or emotional — to be had. It was more remarkable to him that he kept loving Rich. Not because Rich was difficult to love — he wasn't — but just because, even though people fought and feared change, they also craved it, and his love for Rich continued to be enough despite that.

Rudy also knew Rich wasn't especially intimate with his own inner life. He ranted about Rudy's being away at work too much, but he didn't recognize his own restless distractibility. If Rich hadn't been yelling about the catering business, Rudy knew he'd be up in arms about something else, probably involving their relationship, just because it was the easiest target. Rich had lost his stomach for Manhattan, for the deaths, the pace, the competition, the expense, the sheer level of paranoia that was necessary for daily survival — paranoia that made for jokes for midwestern comics but was ignored by New Yorkers at their own peril. Rudy had agreed to move to as remote a place as this because he did not want a suburban life, a life on the outskirts of New York, where you pressed your nose to the glass occasionally to see the real thing. If they were to step off the carousel, Rudy wanted off totally.

And yet, Rich hadn't planned a thing for his retirement, Rudy knew. He had imagined that, like on vacation, amusements and diversions would present themselves. Rich may have thought he wanted Rudy to sit by his side every day till boredom descended like cashmere suffocation, but Rudy knew Rich would hate it if it actually came to pass. They were used to loving each other after twenty years, they preferred each other to everyone else. But it was not an activity on its own.

Whatever it was that Rich did last night, Rudy was prepared to ignore it. Rich would settle down according to his own schedule, whether or not Rudy gave up his catering. The waiting it out would be rough, but it was unavoidable.

28

*T*here were never enough broken appliances, stuck drains or shorted light switches to make Mac Maxwell forget his grief.

Today's job was a loudly humming refrigerator, no doubt a drooping pan or a belt about to give out. Mac could tell that the husband was irritated that his wife hadn't trusted him to do the repair himself, had insisted instead on calling someone in. Mac advertised his services as a handyman, virtually without competition, in the Lakeside Leisure *Leaflet*.

The husband hovered beside him, determined to at least perform a meaningful assist. The wife had smiled sweetly at him when she answered the door, then vanished. Mac recognized the retreat. He knew his being a widower scared some people who'd rather not think about the inevitable.

The kitchen smelled of last night's tomato sauce and this morning's fresh bread, and Mac inhaled both appreciatively. A missed cluster of crumbs sat on a corner of the tablecloth. Water-speckled breakfast dishes were on the drainboard. He noticed every sign of ordinary life because, for the last two years, he'd known none of it. His own kitchen was barren, shut down, dormant. He never used it now; it had been Dorothy's domain.

He scrambled to get down on his side in front of the refrigerator, pulled off the grill, and shone the beam of his flashlight underneath. Sure enough, there was the drain pan, kissing the floor. Nothing that tightening a few screws couldn't take care of.

"I'll have this fixed for you in a jiffy, sir," Mac said to the husband, whose shoes and pant cuffs were all he could see at the moment.

"I coulda done it, I knew it," the husband said.

"Well, I appreciate the work," Mac said, knowing that if the man felt he was doing a good deed, or doing his part to keep the economy in motion, he could rationalize his wife's not having trusted him.

"Bet you keep busy—somebody's probably always got something busted somewhere."

"You got that right," Mac said, grunting a little with the effort of turning the screws at the odd angle he had to approach them.

He finished quickly and hoisted himself off the floor. That was the hardest part, these days, getting vertical again after he'd been bent over or lying down. "I'll just leave you this bill. You can mail me a check," Mac said. The husband shook his hand.

"Oh wait, Mr. Maxwell," the wife came scurrying in to say. She was short and round with pretty blue eyes and soft silver hair. He liked women who didn't dye their hair. Dorothy never did, and she always looked beautiful to him.

"Mac, ma'am," he said.

She smiled. "I made you a loaf of bread." She held it out wrapped in wax paper.

"Well, I sure do appreciate it, ma'am," he said, afraid to take his eyes off the plump brown offering, afraid to meet her eyes.

"Millie," she said.

He smiled, took it under his arm, and headed down the walk to his car. He couldn't hear them talking, the husband and wife, but he could imagine what they were saying. Poor man. All alone now. How long is it his wife is dead? Two years already. Lord have mercy.

He started the car. He had another job at the other end of the community. He might stop and get a plate of something first. He'd heard that some new place — Rudy's, he thought — had good take-out for lunch.

People's sympathy — pity, really, because it always involved a little prayer for themselves — didn't interest him. He wasn't aware himself anymore of feeling grief. There was no joy to contrast it with, so how would he notice? The way he felt reminded him of an eclipse he'd seen one day when he was a young man, still in his thirties. It was a rare one — who knew what kind? He had sat outside on a bench during his lunch hour, careful not to look directly at it the way the papers warned, but just waiting to see what would happen.

118

When it came, the sky stayed a robust, summer blue, but there was no glow. Shadows still fell, but they seemed to have no source. There was an absence of light — not darkness, just the sunlight removed.

That was how he had felt, ever since Dorothy had died. And he didn't expect it to get any better. Not anymore.

29

*F*elicia barely gave Bunny a chance to open her front door before she pushed past her and stomped into the living room.

"Bunny Seagirt, I always knew you were meaner than a hosed-down hornet's nest," she announced. "But you always kept your meanness to yourself. Now you've gone over the line." Felicia scanned the living room for evidence of—what? She half expected a war room complete with a strategic map, but all she saw was that blasted telescope, aimed out the back window.

"Well, and good morning to you, too, Felicia," Bunny said, sauntering over to the couch and reaching for a half empty mug on the coffee table. She was still in her chiffon lounging robe, a not terribly modest garment. Felicia thought, frankly, that she looked debauched. "The decline of civility in our community is really becoming epidemic," Bunny said lazily.

"If it is, you have only yourself to blame," Felicia said. "How can you justify this yellow-bellied witch hunt you're running?"

Bunny scowled. "I don't know what you're talking about, I'm *sure.*"

"This hateful petition, Bunny. Don't play dumb. Everybody's arguing about it. In the market. At the druggist."

"Oh, yes?" Bunny said, one eyebrow cocked. "And what are they saying? Things more sensible than you, I hope. Things about the importance of protecting our investments here in Lakeside Leisure without a bunch of Yankee queers dragging us down. What are you going to do, Felicia — march in support of the first topless homosexual pride march they decide to throw?"

"Bunny, where are you getting this half-baked, overheated hog's manure from? You don't have a political conviction in your whole spineless body. You're just jealous because these people built bigger houses than yours."

"I *am* not," Bunny said, screeching in high C. "Besides, they have more money because they've got no kids. I am proud to have raised a beautiful son in the great, normal, God-fearing American tradition. What have these lesbos given back? They're just a bunch of selfish, sex-crazed sickies."

"First of all, I know for a fact that at least one of them has kids. And besides, Helen is a nicer woman than you by six times and a half and I don't care if you've given birth to the Messiah himself!"

"Fe*li*cia!" Bunny jumped to her feet, sending her coffee mug across the glass tabletop like a skipping stone, leaving a series of cracks in its wake. "You are blas*phem*ing! You are being *brain*washed by these social outcasts!" She surveyed the wreckage of her tabletop. "And *look* what you've made me do! I'll make you pay for this!"

"We're all going to pay for what you're doing, Bunny. But I plan to stop you. Somehow." Felicia scowled around the living room, shaking with rage. "And take *that*," she said, running over and kicking Bunny's telescope to the floor. Bunny started shrieking like a ferret in a steel trap, and Felicia slammed the front door behind her as hard as she could against the sound.

30

*K*aren hadn't allowed Georgia to see how the portrait was coming, and she was having a hard time judging it herself. There was the Georgia she saw with her eyes and the Georgia she had an image of in her head, and somehow she had to make them come together on the canvas.

Georgia was on the stool where she'd been posing for the last three weekends. Karen made her brush her hair out long and wild and wrap herself in a crimson silk shroud she had picked out for just this sitting. It was the right look, snaking around her shoulders and down one exposed leg; she didn't want Georgia in any ordinary outfit. She wanted her to look robed, like some haphazard royalty.

They worked at Georgia's house on Saturday,

Hank's golf afternoon. Karen had explained to Chris that she'd found a model to sit for her, but she didn't say who. Her gut told her that Chris would be jealous.

"Oh, Karen, breaktime, my back is aching," Georgia said, stepping down from the stool and hugging the shroud around her. "You want a lemonade or something?"

"No, I'm fine," Karen said, reluctantly putting down her brush. "But maybe you want to take something with yours to keep from getting too stiff. Aspirin or something." Georgia had her head ducked into the refrigerator. Her bare shoulders were peeking out from above the crimson silk. "Or maybe you should let me get a few kinks out. Where's it hurt? Your neck? Your lower back?"

Georgia carried her glass of lemonade into the living room and settled on the black-and-white speckled couch. "Oh yes, this is much more like it. Not that instrument of torture you're making me sit on," Georgia said. "Are you sure you wouldn't want to do one called Woman Slouching?"

"Nice try," Karen said. "But really, let me see where the knots are. I need you to sit for another hour. Then I might really be close to finished. Or at least to the point where I can work on my own."

"Good, because then you can get back to painting some scenes I can sell. Oh, God — that feels wonderful," Georgia said, dropping her head forward as Karen, standing behind her, worked her fingers along the back of Georgia's neck.

"Why didn't you say something sooner, if you were so cramped?" Karen asked, but Georgia just grunted for her to continue. *Don't get stupid,* Karen admonished herself as she firmly pressed her fingers along Georgia's shoulders. Her skin was the color of vanilla, some shade past ivory but just short of maize, and Karen had mixed paint for days to get the tone just right. But now, with the heat and smoothness of Georgia's skin right under her fingertips, Karen couldn't pretend her interest was strictly artistic. She felt a pulse begin between her legs and a splash of heat rush at her throat. A fist of pressure lodged itself against her diaphragm.

Don't be an idiot, she told herself again, taking a deep, arid breath. And yet there was Georgia, relaxed beneath her touch, her breathing having gone more shallow. She was not fleeing, or telling her to stop, or prompting idle conversation. She seem concentrated and still, obedient to the rhythms of Karen's hands. Karen moved her fingers up Georgia's scalp, luxuriating in the feel of Georgia's baby-fine hair tickling the back of her hands and wrists. The heat spilled down Karen's thighs; she felt herself grow moist, and knew she would soon be lost to instinct.

"God," Georgia breathed. Her shoulders went slack, and with it, the crimson silk slid partway down her shoulders, baring the tops of her breasts and the dark finger of her cleavage. Karen's throat was dry, her legs no longer reliable. She sagged to her knees behind the couch, her lips and nose just inches from Georgia's hair, her neck, that slope of shoulders. Karen was in a full-blown panic, and she cursed the very bad handicap of not being able to see Georgia's face or eyes, to know if she were merely in the trusting repose of massage, or if this was permission to be seduced.

Finally, the decision was taken from her. Something

like hunger pressed Karen forward and she slid her hands, open-palmed, under the cool silk shroud and watched it fall into a crimson puddle around Georgia's waist. Georgia's full, freckled breasts were in Karen's hands, the nipples upright between her fingers. She pulled Georgia's earlobe between her teeth, licked the arc of her ear, moved her parted lips down the side of Georgia's neck, her throat, all the while stroking with light fingertips Georgia's dark, straining nipples.

"*Karen!* " Georgia whispered harshly.

Karen leapt away. "I'm so sorry — forgive me." The room tilted and a ferocious surge of shame and terror swept over her.

"Get over here," Georgia ordered, roughly seizing Karen's wrist and wresting her over to the front of the couch, pulling her down beside her. Karen was shocked silent as Georgia took her face in her hands and drew her close. The kiss was as new as adolescence; Georgia was sucking on her hard and long, without pause. Karen felt as if the top of her head were pumped with helium, as if her eyes might float right out of her skull if she didn't keep them pressed tightly shut. So many physical sensations were flooding her that she could barely register her amazement at the circumstances. Together, they wrestled off Georgia's panties, and Karen gently tipped Georgia onto her back on the couch, sliding off it to again kneel, this time alongside Georgia.

They stayed locked in their kiss, like a conversation, swimming through thoughts and words, their strokes nearly synchronized. Karen loved the taste of Georgia — something cinnamony and caramel — and Karen felt as if a raw strip had opened up from her throat to her groin, and she could feel the wind rushing through her. *Wait, don't hurry her,* Karen warned herself, and yet she didn't see how she could hold off. She longed, at the very edge of begging, for Georgia to touch her, to fill her up, to get inside her, but she didn't dare ask, didn't dare assume that Georgia wanted her, too.

Karen steeled herself. She feared that at any moment Georgia might realize what was happening, might just as soon kill her as kiss her, but the sense of trespass was swept aside by another wave of longing. She reached for Georgia's breasts, soft and overripe; to Karen they felt like the essence of sex. Further down Karen's hand went, over Georgia's hip, down to a soft thigh; all the while she was mesmerized by their own kissing, the wetness of their lips and tongues and breath together. And then her fingers tripped over the damp and coiled hair between Georgia's legs, and parted it. She let her fingers enter and rise, pressing against warmth and darkness, and fought the urge to roar, from the need to do more, to have more, of Georgia. She felt so greedy for Georgia, for the sheer, ripping escape of climax, that she had to fight not to touch herself, too, to trade some release for some measure of sanity.

Georgia's arms clapped around Karen's back, and Karen felt her following her thrusts. She let her thumb ride the small, slippery shaft that was making Georgia writhe. Georgia broke from their kiss and panted at Karen's shoulder, cursing in low, angry whispers — *God*-damn it, God-*damn* it. The air between them had grown humid and thick, alive with sighs and creaking. Georgia wrestled up to a sitting position, and Karen felt a sharp pressure at her wrist, as if it might snap, and worried that the wetness was dripping onto the couch, and they would be found out and punished and shamed. But Georgia seemed unconcerned about it all. She was squeezing Karen's head, and bucking against her, and making a frightening, angry sound that Karen had never heard and yet recognized. Then all at once Georgia went rigid and still, and fell limply against Karen. Karen let her, even though her own knees were crackling with pain, and her own groin was throbbing petulantly, until Georgia's breathing slowed and returned to normal.

Georgia pulled away just enough that they were looking directly at each other, for the first time in what felt like hours. "I'm so sorry," was all Karen could think of to say. And she was: No matter what Georgia insisted, Karen herself knew that she had been the aggressor, the seducer, knew that she had taken advantage, had known what she might do and tried to get away with it. She had complicated their friendship and betrayed Chris, maybe more than could be forgiven. Her eyes welled hot with tears and she shut them, sending one tear racing down to the corner of her mouth.

Georgia was silent. She hugged Karen's waist with her thighs, and slowly tugged the paint-stained T-shirt over Karen's head. Karen fell mute, too, though she wanted to stop her, stop this. Still, she didn't resist, couldn't resist, as Georgia unzipped her jeans and pushed them and her underwear to the floor. Karen kept her eyes on Georgia's full, rocking breasts, the skin damp with their efforts, the dark nipples puckered. Georgia pulled Karen to her, so their breasts were flush, and with both hands, pushed Karen's legs apart. Karen sagged onto Georgia's shoulders as she felt the unexpected explosion of fingers, inside her and out, running, galloping fingers, thrusting and beating, circling and probing, till Karen was reeling and came, once, and then, after just a moment's rest, again. When it was over, she cried into Georgia's neck, and felt Georgia's fingers, sticky on her back.

"Shhhh, shhhhh, *shhhh,*" Georgia was breathing into her ear. "What *are* you crying about? Or do you always cry after you come?" Georgia helped her up from her knees onto the couch.

"What are we doing?" Karen asked, moved anew by Georgia's face and how beautiful she thought she was. "And that was *not* your first time with a woman, you goddamned liar," she said, not angry, just surprised. She was fighting to control a slight tremor in her arms and legs.

Georgia lay back on the couch, her legs across Karen's lap. She rescued the crimson shroud from the floor and tossed it over both of them. "I am not a liar. You just never asked." She smiled playfully.

Karen figured this must be how it feels to be hustled. "Well, I'm asking you now."

Georgia looped one arm behind her head. "It was when I was first married. Hank was hardly ever home. A friend of mine from college had moved to Atlanta and we started spending a lot of time together. We'd get drunk and do silly stuff like play strip poker, or she'd pretend to be Hank or I'd pretend to be her old boyfriend and we'd . . . start, I don't know . . . playing." She laughed. "Well. Later she confessed she'd been a lesbian for years, and that she was in love with me and oh, it was a big mess. I'd enjoyed it. Women, I think, are probably better lovers than men, on the whole, but I was crazy in love with Hank. I was grateful to her, for her, whatever—but I was not in love. Still, I liked knowing that about myself, that I could be with a woman, too."

"What happened? With her, I mean?" Across the decades, Karen felt empathy for this other lesbian, whoever she was.

"The whole thing lasted all of four months, and when she realized I wasn't leaving Hank, she moved away. We didn't stay in touch."

"Did you ever tell Hank?"

"Oh God, no. And I'm sure there are things he's never told me, and we're happier for it, I'd guess."

Karen felt drained, numb. "Did you plan this, today?"

"No. Absolutely not. But—" here Georgia looked away "—I don't think you realize how you look at me when you're painting. Today I really saw it and I still had no intention, not a shred of it—God, affairs are so messy and complicated—but when you put your hands on my neck, I just...well, I think I remembered."

"Ah." Karen nodded, meaninglessly. She felt seasick. She didn't like learning *after* lovemaking how little she knew about her lover. "Well."

Georgia gripped Karen's hand. "But tell me why you were crying."

Karen shook her head. "I don't really know. I don't think I can say. But I do know, and I think you do, too, that we won't repeat this."

"No, far better not to," Georgia said, gathering her shroud around her. She leaned over and kissed Karen on the cheek. "I'll meet you on the stool. Take your time." And then she left the couch.

Karen sat stock-still, naked, for how long she didn't know, trying to figure out how to explain to Georgia that there was no way now she could finish the portrait.

31

*H*appiness, Lara had discovered, was a physical sensation. When it announced itself, as it was now, in a tickle around the ribs or a pleasant pressure behind the eyes, she paused to savor it. It was eight thirty-nine, according to the digital clock, and she was in bed next to Helen. The sun was still shy, the sky more white than blue, but brightness lit their beige sheets and walls. The window was on Helen's side, the side Helen chose in every house they'd ever lived in, every hotel room they'd ever slept in. That was the rule, and it struck Lara as remarkable that they had stuck by it so faithfully all this time.

Helen was still asleep, her eyelids twitching with some dream she might share if she woke soon, her hair twisted wildly, as always, as if she had spent the long night pulling at it. Lara had loved other women, mostly before, but a few during her early years with Helen. She had found it harder to settle down than Helen had, and Helen had had the grace to be tolerant. Lara wasn't sure she recognized it as grace at the time, but now, thirty-five years later, she knew that's what it had been.

The other women . . . Lara occasionally thought of them even now. One had been much older and was now dead, a fact that startled and scared her every time it occurred to her. The two others that she counted as significant she had now lost complete track of, something she once would never have thought possible. But it was as if the string connecting them had, over the decades, reeled out farther and farther, till all the tension gave way, and they were gone.

When Lara thought of them now, they seemed less like people than pressed flowers, or little parables she might have learned in childhood. None of them were as real or particular or complicated or good as Helen. Sometimes she thought that was just the function of memory, flattening and diminishing landscapes as it went. Memory, after all, was always unreliable, even in youth; by her age, it was downright treacherous. Still, most of the time she trusted the conclusion: that Helen was just better, and better for her, than anyone else in the world. In fact, she had come full circle on this point. When she was very young, she had believed that there was one other person preordained for everyone, and you must spend your life searching out just that person. Later she dismissed that idea with a snort, chalked up its quaint romanticism to adolescence. Now she was not so sure. It was hard enough to spend your own life well, let alone shared with another person, so when it was accomplished, who dared say the pairing had been purely random?

She watched Helen's eyelids: they were smooth and still. Maybe she would wake up soon. Lara studied Helen's cheeks and chin, her neck and earlobes. She had known this face when it was twenty-five, when they were invincible and effortlessly toned and tireless. Today they were both almost old women, and she loved Helen just as much — no, truly, more — because they had each been through their own restlessness, disappointment, even disgust, and still came through it deciding the other was worth it. She looked at Helen now and was glad they'd hidden out here; New York was no place for old ladies. It was hardly a place for young ladies, but at least once they'd had the energy to slog every day through the fear and the danger, the chaos and the rotten weather. She felt, down here, safe in a foxhole. They were among their own kind — if not the gay kind, at least the old and the nearly old, and that was an important sorority, too. This was where they belonged.

Helen's eyes squinted open. She gave Lara a thin smile and a lazy hug. "Good morning," Lara said, kissing the tip of Helen's nose.

"I was dreaming," Helen said, her voice unpracticed for the day. "I was back at work. A woman came to me and wanted me to train and show her Yorkie. And I said, I can't, I do spaniels. And then I said, Look at that dog — I've eaten meals bigger than that dog!"

They both burst out laughing, Lara tucking herself under Helen's arm as Helen rolled onto her back. "Well," Lara said, "either you went to bed hungry, or you miss work."

"Probably a little of both. Do you still miss work terribly?"

Under the sheets, Lara put one leg over Helen's leg. "I thought my work was important, but I didn't love it, not like you loved yours." She flashed on an image of herself in her office, the one she had worked so hard to get to, the one she was so proud of and a little vain about, the corner office, the partner's office, the one the young associates whisked by on their first days and were a little terrified of. "Some days, I remember, I'd be so stressed, I wondered if I had some kind of Tourette's syndrome. Because I'd be so wired that, no matter where I was — the person in the car in front of me, or on the bank line — they'd be doing something that enraged me, and I'd think, Dumb shit. Stupid fuck. Crazy son of a bitch. I was always on the brink of hating everybody."

"I know," Helen said. "And you'd come home, and it would take you an hour before you weren't oozing adrenaline out of every pore."

"Oh God," Lara said, "and remember when I was going through menopause and I had those couple of months when I'd been at the office and in court so much that I was getting only a few hours sleep a night? And I actually put the music from *Psycho* on my machine at work, with the message, Hi, This is Lara Gallagher. Leave your message, and just don't piss me off."

Helen's whole face crinkled in a silent, hearty laugh. "Of course I remember. The first time I got your tape I was horrified. I thought someone had played a joke on you — and then you told me you did it yourself. I couldn't *believe* it!"

"My dark side. Few know the truth but you."

"Thank God," Helen said, reaching up to tousle Lara's hair. "My little beast."

Lara wriggled closer. The sky had turned baby blue, and the sun was warm on her eyelids. Happiness fluttered up to her throat and left her speechless.

32

When the phone rang, Rich answered it. He almost always did now. Rudy was forever answering the phone at the store so when it rang at the house, he waved his hands wildly, as if scalded, warning Rich that he wouldn't pick it up. He was out in the backyard now, anyway, poking at the bushes, contemplating new landscaping schemes.

"This is Greg," the voice on the other end said matter of factly. Rich felt a ribbon of heat snake up from his groin.

"And this is Rich," he said, figuring that Greg's terse greeting was for caution's sake, in the event that, if someone answering didn't respond to the name, he could easily hang up. "How did you find me?"

"You showed me your license. You're listed."

Rich smiled, hearing Greg's voice soften, relax, now that their identities were confirmed. "I'm glad."

"Are you?" Greg asked.

"Sure. Now I don't have to hang out at that tacky bar again, just waiting to run into you."

"But you live with someone, don't you?" Greg asked.

"Why do you think that?"

"No one moves to your part of town alone."

"I could have been widowed."

"You didn't seem like it. You seemed . . . too content."

"Maybe I was a happy widow." Rich regretted his words instantly, as he watched Rudy go by the kitchen window. It was a pre-plague joke he hadn't been able to completely shake off, long after such a notion wasn't even remotely lighthearted.

"But you're not, are you?" Greg said.

"No, not the widow part."

"Does that mean we can't see each other again?"

Rich felt his hairline go damp. He hadn't thought about Greg in the week since he'd seen him . . . not really, except for one morning in the shower when he'd wondered briefly who the boy was and what his life was about. Now that Greg's voice was humming in his ear, Rich realized he did want to see him, he would love to see him. But he didn't want to do this to Rudy. Not now. Not anymore.

"Are you still there?" Greg asked.

"It'd be great to see you," Rich said, a slow swirl of arousal clouding his judgment. "I just don't see how — or where."

"You could come here." Greg gave him an address

and directions, explaining that it was about forty-five minutes away.

"And *you* don't live with someone? I imagined parents, or a wife."

"A wife? Really. You took me for a husband?" Greg said.

"Well, an unhappy husband."

"Definitely not the husband part."

"Ah."

"Can you get away Friday night? Around seven?" Greg asked.

Certain moments about their night together had freeze-framed in Rich's memory: looking up to see Greg's handsome face over his shoulder at the bar. Tugging the gleaming white briefs off his hips. There was no good reason to start this up. But Friday night, he knew Rudy had a party to cater. A seventieth birthday. "It happens I can get away," Rich said. He heard the front door open. "Thanks for calling," he said, hanging up.

"Who was that?" Rudy asked, coming in and throwing open the refrigerator.

"Someone selling an alarm system."

"Now don't go getting one just so it feels to you like back home," Rudy said.

"Good point," Rich said. All kinds of old habits, he realized, died hard.

33

*B*unny was studying the catering menu when a short, swarthy bald man approached from behind the counter.

"I'm Rudy," the man said. "Any questions at all, just give a shout." He smiled, and then bustled away to wait on the first of the gathering lunch crowd.

The little storefront was sweetly decorated, Bunny noted — its red, white and black tile and cozy glass tables made the place feel homey and sophisticated at the same time. Tantalizing smells swirled above her head, and customers were dispatched with an air of cheerful competence. Hunger warmed Bunny's stomach.

The menu was pricier than she would have liked. But after all, her son didn't have a birthday every day. Especially a birthday he consented to spend with his parents. It was a special occasion, and Bunny was sure he must have some kind of announcement. A girl. A decision about a career. He'd never made a secret of hating her cooking, and, when he visited, had mercilessly criticized every restaurant they'd ever brought him to, so she resigned herself to bringing food in. It was Bill's idea. He'd heard good things about this new place.

The man — Rudy, the owner, she supposed — returned and smiled at her expectantly.

"I'm having a small dinner party," she told him. "Is four too small for you?" She figured she'd count on one extra just in case he arrived with a fiancée.

"Not at all," he said. "When is this for?"

"In three weeks. And I have to tell you, I'm really at a loss here. It's my son's birthday. He's just graduated from college — New York University — and I just don't know his taste in food these days." She felt herself blushing as the man nodded and murmured sympathetically. He was a handsome man, despite his shiny head, and his voice resonated in a way that made her as tingly as a school girl.

"Why don't you leave it to me?" he said. "Just tell me your price range, and whether anyone has any dietary restrictions, and I'll make you a feast to remember."

Bunny wasn't used to someone with an East Coast accent being so solicitous. "Well, I don't know . . ."

"I'll tell you what. Since this is such an intimate affair and your guest of honor is obviously a man with a discriminating palate, I can even whip up some dishes that aren't on my regular menu. Something really special — maybe a pumpkin or lobster ravioli to start, then maybe a grouper in phyllo with asparagus

141

spears. Or, if you want pasta as the main dish, we could start with an arugula and Parmesan salad and then do a penne with ricotta, shredded chicken and red peppers —"

"My goodness! I didn't realize I'd have so many options." Still, her instinct was to trust him, and so she agreed.

"Oh, I live in Lakeside Leisure, too," Rudy said as Bunny was giving him her address.

"Really? You're new then. What street are you on?"

"Paxton Court."

Bunny felt herself go clammy all over. She got lightheaded and staggered back a few steps.

"Ma'am, are you okay?" he said, rushing out from behind the counter and sliding a chair underneath her.

"Oh, I'm fine, just a little . . . warm all of a sudden."

"Sherry, get me a glass of water," Rudy commanded one of the helpers. The glass materialized instantly and he handed it over.

"Thank you," she said, sipping. "I'll be just fine, now. Just the heat getting to me."

"Can I have someone give you a lift home?" he asked, eyeing her with obvious concern.

Bunny swallowed a few more gulps. "No, no, I've got my car. But thanks just the same."

"Why don't I give you a call in a couple of days and go over the menu I've put together for you?"

"Yes, good idea," Bunny said. And she got up and hurried out the door.

34

*A*re you coming to bed soon?" Chris asked, leaning against the doorway of the sun room Karen used as a studio.

"That sounds like a good idea," Karen said, putting her brush down and pulling off her paint smock. "I think I'm doing more harm than good now anyway."

Chris was surprised, but pleasantly. Ever since Karen had sold a painting, she'd been pushing herself to do more, and more ambitious paintings. And the busier she got, the more pro bono work Chris took on. In fact, Chris had spent the day two hours away at a university library, researching the history of a plot of land that both developers and environmental protectionists wanted. It was getting to be where she and

Karen were seeing each other as little as they did before retiring.

Karen stripped efficiently in front of her closet, and then threw back the blanket on her side. "God, I didn't realize how tired I was," she said as her head sank into the pillows doubled up against the brass headboard.

Chris smiled across the room as she neatly folded her own clothes. She'd been single most of her life, coupled only on and off. Single long enough, certainly, to still have a grain of awe left for the fact that this graceful woman now fell asleep and woke up next to her in bed every night and day.

Chris went around the room with a book of matches, lighting the clusters of tall, spindly candles they had arranged on their dressers and night tables. When she was finished, the room glowed like a cave lit by moonlight. She lay down on the cool, cotton sheets next to Karen, and reached out for her.

"Goodnight, lover," Karen said, leaning over to give Chris a peck.

"I miss you," Chris said, running her hand down Karen's side, over the slope of hip and down her thigh.

"Me, too, but I'm half asleep already. Tomorrow," she said.

Chris rolled onto her back and watched the tiny flames lap at the darkness. She stared into the small halos of light, watching their slow-motion dance for a while, not feeling in the least sleepy. She got up to blow them all out, then padded back through the darkened house into the sun room.

She switched on the standing lamp next to the wicker lounge chair and sat down to consider Karen's latest landscape on the easel. It was too early to judge how it might turn out but she liked sitting here, anyway, among Karen's canvases. She imagined that the air vibrated with Karen's energy, as if her essence were released into the air after so much time spent here. Chris felt closer to her here, where she had spent the efforts of her spirit, than she did sometimes next to her in bed, where her sleep was a blankness, an absence.

She shivered a little; it was a cool night and she was naked. She hugged her arms to herself and went over to the far wall to flip through the canvases leaning there. The first few were untouched, the next few were painted all one color, either abandoned or being saved for future. And then there was the unfamiliar portrait.

As soon as Chris saw it, she admitted to herself that she had been looking for it. Not just because Karen made such light of it and claimed to know so little about the model, but because she wouldn't let Chris see it, protesting that it was terrible, an embarrassment.

In fact the portrait was the best work Karen had ever done, in Chris's estimation. The woman in the painting looked strong, warm, wise, sensual. A mass of dark, wispy curls fell over one shoulder and, amid a wrap of crimson, one breast was haphazardly exposed. The whole mood of the portrait was smoky and erotic. Looking at it, Chris felt like a voyeur. Seeing it, she knew the painting had been a labor of love.

"I'm sorry," Karen said, in the doorway suddenly, the bedsheet wrapped around her. "I should have shown it to you."

Chris jumped, slapping her hand to her chest and making the dumb, startled cry of a trapped animal. "How long have you been standing there?"

"Long enough to know you're upset with me."

"You were going to do my portrait," Chris said. She hated how she sounded: ridiculous, childish.

"I still am."

Chris looked back at the painting. "It's very fine work. Your best. You must know that." She looked it over more closely and realized the bottom was raw yet, and the background largely unconsidered. She looked up at Karen. "It's not finished, though, is it?"

"Not quite. But it will be. Soon."

Chris nodded and put the portrait down carefully, afraid, anymore, to meet Karen's eyes. "I'll try to be patient," she said finally. And she went over, put her arm around Karen, and walked her back to bed.

35

*A*ngie was parked in her Range Rover across the street from Bunny Seagirt's house. She didn't exactly have a plan, but she was sure she could hatch one given enough time. To be on the safe side, she had stocked the car with binoculars, a camera and tape recorder, and was wearing a long, blond wig she had bought for the occasion and her big, wraparound sun glasses from her motorcycle days. The getup was hot as hell, so she had to keep the air-conditioning blasting.

It was another blazingly sunny Florida day, the kind, Angie was sure, that was unhealthy to be out in for even a few minutes. People complained that the weather was lousy up north, crime made it dangerous, stress made it deadly, but no one in New York, she was willing to bet, was dropping dead of skin cancer the way she bet they were down here.

Angie found herself making all kinds of comparisons between down here and up there since she'd retired and moved away. She hadn't expected to miss New York, but now it was winning points for all kinds of things it wouldn't have occurred to her to count when she lived there. Lack of skin cancer was one. For another, at least when you were terrorized and pissed off all day long — for example, stepping over the homeless and hating them for messing up your sidewalk but also hating yourself for not helping — you weren't in danger of dying of boredom.

Besides, she missed teaching. That was a shock. She had spent so much time when she was a professor privately berating her students for being lazy-minded, TV-drugged, shallow automatons that, she figured now, she'd stopped seeing that she had liked them for their malleability, their freshness, their irreverence. And she had gotten to spend a lifetime in the unreal circumstance of being paid to believe that the classics mattered, that they could change lives, that preserving their meaning was important to the culture.

She clicked on the radio, put her head back. What's more, back home, bigots like Bunny Seagirt did not last long. They found the air impossible to breathe after a while, and slunk back to whatever backwater they had been born in. Because New York was a place teeming, fairly choking on diversity, you'd have been hard pressed to find a majority of anything, to figure out who was aberrant. Angie wanted that back. She hated the rigid, self-conscious way her face froze when confronted with people like Bunny. Because even after a lifetime of being out, of marching in marches and

148

rallying at rallies, it took only one Bunny Seagirt to make her feel oppressed and freakish all over again.

Angie heard the hum of a garage door lifting and looked over to see that it was at Bunny Seagirt's house. A Cadillac was backing out, and she put the Range Rover into gear.

She followed at a safe distance, even letting the occasional car come between them. She was close enough now to see that the driver was a man; Bunny's husband, no doubt. Fine, so she'd see what he was up to. He drove to the far end of the community, the older, less grand part, and pulled to the curb. She stopped far behind him and grabbed for the binoculars — and was stunned to see that the man she found with her magnified vision was the masher from the supermarket and the pool!

She watched him walk up the path of the house and knock on the door. When a woman answered, he went in.

Angie's mind raced. If this was as bad — or as good, was what she meant — as it looked, she had many succulent options. She could storm this house now and catch him in his adulterous act. She could drive back to Bunny's and offer to show her where her husband was. She could wait and confront Mr. Bunny Seagirt as he walked out the door. But she'd have to think it over carefully as she waited for him to reemerge. Whatever way she went, though, she was pretty sure she'd found the way to bring the purple posse to its knees.

36

*T*oday's call came from Paxton Court, and Mac knew what that meant.

He'd lived in small towns his whole life, and Lakeside Leisure was just a modern version, no different in critical ways. Everyone loved to talk about everyone else, and everyone liked to peck to death those who were different. Of course, the rumor mill got a big head start thanks to Bunny Seagirt going door-to-door, yabbering about the pervert menace to property values. Mac wasn't quick to anger but she'd ticked him off, and he'd chased her off his front stoop. He was no homo rights rabble-rouser, either, but her tactics offended his belief that a man's land was his own.

It had been Dorothy's idea to move to this

retirement village, not his. He hadn't wanted to leave his own house, his own backyard. But she didn't want him taxing his heart raking and edging and mowing. Better to be somewhere where they took care of the grounds all for you, she'd said. And that's how cruel life could be. She was the one who'd died.

The woman who answered the door at the lavender house was small and fine boned with loose, light brown curls. She smiled at him, her eyes crinkling into crescents, as if she'd just been told a good joke. Given what he'd heard about female homosexuals, he was surprised at how sweet-looking and pretty she was. She put out her hand just as a graceful spaniel bounded forward and carefully sniffed his kneecaps.

"You must be Mac. We're Helen and Emma," the woman said, gesturing him in.

"Which is which?" he asked, confused.

She laughed, a contagious sound that made him happy, an unexpected jolt. "Excuse me — *I'm* Helen," she said. "I should mind Emma's manners and get her to introduce herself more often."

"She looks about smart enough to do it, ma'am," Mac said, kneeling down and taking the dog's head in his hands and massaging her ears. Her coat was satiny, and her pudding-dark eyes searched his with sympathy and trust.

"Dog people, are you?" Helen asked.

"Used to have a farm."

"That explains it," she said.

And because she seemed to be waiting, he nearly added, Used to have a wife, too. And a reason to get up in the morning. But he checked himself, and stood up. "So you've got a loose window thing-a-ma-jig, you said on the tape."

151

"Yes, and here's the thing-a-ma-jig in question," she said, pulling what looked like a hair clip out of her shorts pocket. "I found it on the floor under the frame, and now the window flies up and down without any tension. This one, right over here in the living room."

"Hmmm." He took the unassuming-looking piece from her. "These new windows . . . ," he said, inspecting everything methodically. He hadn't ever installed this kind, and he wasn't at all sure he was going to be able to help her. He opened and shut the window, played with the locks, tilted it in, all the while holding the clip like a key, waiting to poke it into something. Then, unexpectedly, it slid neatly into the horizontal column in the lip, and the resistance returned instantly to the window tracks.

"That appears to have done the trick," he said. "Another strenuous day's work."

"Oh — that's terrific!" she said, pulling and pushing the window up and down like a kid with a new toy. "What do I owe you? Is a check okay or —"

"No charge, ma'am. This one's on me."

"Out of the question. Just because it was easy, doesn't mean you didn't do a real service. You absolutely must accept payment," she said, disappearing into another room and returning with her checkbook.

"I'd really rather you do it my way, ma'am," he said. He saw her hesitate and knew that he had to give her some way to reciprocate. "But I'll tell you what. I'll take a glass of iced tea for my trouble — if you let us call it even."

"Okay, then," she said, and led him into the kitchen. "But you also have to stop calling me ma'am." Sunlight streamed in through the large window, and plants hung in the corners. Everything gleamed white and chrome. She put out an apple pie and plates and sat across from him at the glass table. "I can't tell you how excited I am to have the window fixed. I was imagining cranes coming in and ripping out walls and all kinds of nightmares."

"So was I, for a minute there."

The springer joined them, her toenails clicking on the white tile as she walked over. She sat at his feet, her nostrils flexing in the direction of the pie.

"Emma, no begging," Helen warned. "She knows better than to do that to me, but she's taking advantage of a newcomer. Emma, come over here."

"It's okay," he said, leaning over to toy with the dog's ears again. "She's such a beautiful animal." And then he listened as Helen told him about her career as a professional dog handler, the traveling, the shows, the getting to know whole families of dogs, the sons and daughters of champions, and how they could be like children, taking the best and worst of their parents, not always in the proportions one would choose. He listened happily, liking her stories, the funny phrases — "show dog and a half" and "a dog that owned the rug" — but also the sound of her voice, the look on her face as she told them. It had been a long time since he'd sat at a kitchen table with a woman and shared a piece of pie and conversation. The exile had been largely of his own making, he knew, since he'd preferred his private memories of Dorothy to anyone he knew or met.

"My wife loved dogs. She babied the ones we had on our farm, and they were barely domesticated."

"Your wife . . . is she . . ."

"She died two years ago," he managed with a

strangled sound. And then the worst happened: hot tears streamed down his face. He clapped his hands over his eyes and rubbed hard, shaking back a sob. He was stiff with humiliation. "Forgive me," he mumbled, starting to rise from his chair.

"Don't be ridiculous," she said, grabbing his wrist forcefully. "Please sit down. I'm the one who's sorry. You must have loved her very much. It's a rare thing. I'm privileged to witness it. I wish I'd had a chance to know her."

He kept his face obscured with his hands, and allowed himself to feel the warm lap of gratitude. He felt the force of her sincerity and it sobered him, awed him even, to have this accidental encounter with kindness. She handed him a napkin and he dutifully blew his nose.

"Thanks for the pie, ma'am — Helen. And you let me know if anything else in the house gives you trouble." He stood, and Emma rose with him. "For that matter, you let me know if anything or anyone *outside* the house gives you trouble, too." He held her gaze until his meaning, about Bunny Seagirt, seemed to dawn on her.

"Ah, yes, well thank you very much for that. I hope I never have to take you up on it."

And as she waved to him from the door, he hoped she never had to, either, even given how much he realized he wanted to see her again.

37

*G*eorgia was glad when the waiter finally brought their meals. She didn't feel much up to talking tonight, and the food was a convenient distraction. She could tell that Felicia was anxious, and disappointed in her for not being her usual chatty self, especially since this was the first time they were out to dinner as a foursome — with Ted and Hank in tow — and she knew Felicia was eager for the outing to be a big success.

"Oh, yours looks scrumptious," Felicia said, gesturing at Georgia's plate, in another attempt to draw her out, Georgia knew. She'd gotten penne in a red sauce and though it looked pretty good, she had no appetite. In fact, the heavy scents commingling in the slightly undercooled restaurant, the clanking of silverware and the buzz of unharmonious conversation in the low-ceilinged room was making her irritable and a little queasy. Hank was doing his usual, viewing his plate with deep suspicion. Whatever he was served, he poked and picked at it as if it might be poisoned. Even ice cubes floating in his drinks were inspected for offending particles that might be trapped inside.

Fortunately she didn't have to worry about drawing him into the conversation. He was always able to hold his own with new people, and he was finding Ted to be his favorite kind of audience: one he could plow over and flatten to the ground for indefinite stretches. Every time Georgia honed in on his monologue, he was regaling Ted with tales of his real-estate selling prowess, of amazing deals done and bad deals undone. Poor Ted, who'd rented all his life until he and Felicia had bought their modest Lakeside Leisure home, was glazing over but struggling, Georgia could tell, to make relevant comments. He didn't realize, Georgia saw, that Hank didn't need any of the usual cues of con-versational encouragement. He considered someone a good listener if they shut up while he talked.

"Hank, honey, maybe Ted doesn't want to hear all the highlights of real estate sales in the tri-state area over the last thirty years," Georgia whispered to him, trying for joviality but still sounding reproachful.

Hank gave her a pinched look but didn't protest, and startled Ted with a sudden question about what he thought would happen to the price of first-class postage in the age of the fax machine.

"So, how is that new painter you signed up doing?" Felicia asked her, nudging Ted to pass the cheese.

This was precisely the subject Georgia was desperate to avoid, but she knew she couldn't be curt to Felicia. Here Felicia was, all dressed up in a pale blue, big-belted dress, with lace trim at the neck and cuffs, waiting with her watery light brown eyes, unwary as a goldfish in a dentist office's tank.

"Oh, well, you know, now that the first painting sold, she's trying to get me more." Georgia could think of nothing else to say that wouldn't betray the tumult she felt whenever her mind drifted to the subject of Karen. She stabbed at her pasta and sent the fork skidding across the plate with a screech. Several drippy pieces of penne went sailing onto the sleeve of her pink silk blouse. "Damn! Excuse me," she said, grabbing her purse and jumping up.

"Here, I'll help you," Felicia said.

"No, Felicia, eat your meal while it's hot. I'll just be a moment," Georgia said, feeling a quiver of rage not just because of the possibly ruined blouse, but because the thought of Karen had put her on the brink of tears. She didn't want to think of Karen, and yet since that day on the couch, she hadn't been able to think of much else.

Georgia elbowed her way past the ambling waiters when she saw that Felicia was sprinting after her on white pumps. Georgia shoved open the bathroom door and was about to plunge her sleeve under the faucet when Felicia screamed.

"No! *Don't!* You'll ruin it!" She grabbed Georgia's arm away as if she were a child about to stick her hand into a fireplace.

"Felicia, really, go eat your meal while it's —"

"Oh, hush," Felicia said with a firmness that surprised Georgia. Felicia was dabbing carefully at the tomato sauce streaks with tissues. "Do you think I give a hen's scratch about the temperature of my meal? I'm not in here to take care of your blouse, though I can

157

see you need that, too. Here," she said, rooting around in her black, shell-shaped pocketbook. "I never go to a restaurant without talcum powder in my purse. Somebody's always spilling something, and you just dab this on and don't brush it off till the morning. I've been doing it since my kids were little, and it's saved me a fortune in dry cleaning bills."

Georgia submitted as Felicia sprinkled the powder and gently blew the excess off. Georgia's own mother was dead fifteen years, and she'd forgotten how soothing it was to be worried over this way. "Thank you, Felicia."

"I'm in here to take care of a friend," Felicia said, looking at her steadily. "I can see something's wrong. What is it? Is it your health? Hank's health?"

"Oh, Felicia, I'm sorry I'm spoiling your night," Georgia said, leaning against the sink. She suddenly craved a cigarette, though she hadn't smoked since she was first married. "No, we're both fit as ever. I'm just a little tired and cranky. Please don't give it a second thought."

Felicia scanned her face with undisguised skepticism. "It's okay if you don't feel you can tell me. But I want you to know if you change your mind, I'm here."

Georgia hugged her arms to her chest and regarded Felicia seriously. She'd always found her company pleasant, but she never thought of her as anyone she could have a real friendship with. But why was that? Because Felicia was older, not stylish, not from the city? And yet here she was, saying the things anyone would want a friend to say. And Georgia had no one, no one at all, to talk to about Karen.

"Well, actually . . ." Georgia said slowly, debating,

158

even as the words were forming in her mouth, if she should change her mind. But she didn't get to the words before she started crying.

"Georgia! Now tell me instantly what it is that's breaking your heart so!" Felicia scooted over next to her and patted the back of her hand lightly.

"Oh, Felicia," Georgia said, trying to press the tears back with the tips of her fingers. "I'm in love with someone else and we can't be together." She covered her eyes with one hand and held onto her stomach with the other.

"Oh, oh, oh," Felicia said, patting her hand. "Oh, oh, oh!"

"It's impossible, just terrible. I wish the feelings would just go away and I could get back to my life."

"Does Hank know?"

"He's clueless. His usual unintuitive self," Georgia said. "But you know, this isn't about him. I have nothing against him. He's my oldest friend. I could never leave him."

"No, no, there, there, of course not," Felicia was saying. Then she pulled her hand away suddenly. "It's not Ted, is it?"

This shocked Georgia into stoicism. She looked hard at Felicia to see if she were joking, and when she saw the blend of fear and dread in her eyes, she struggled not to laugh. Little shuffling bent-over Ted. "Perish the thought, Felicia. How could I do that to you? No, this is someone you don't know."

"I'm sorry, I know that was — oh, it was stupid and selfish of me to ask," Felicia said, moving away from the sink to pace. "I lost my head there for a moment. You know, at my age, we all worry so about —"

"Don't apologize. Ted is a very sweet man, but he

only has eyes for you. Besides, in this case, I'm not an admirer from afar. I'm having an affair with — this person." As soon as Georgia admitted it aloud, she knew she couldn't stay away from Karen the way she had planned.

"What will you do?" Felicia asked, wringing the handle of her purse.

Georgia turned around to the mirror to survey the damage done to her mascara. What would she do, indeed? It was ludicrous to consider continuing the affair, and yet, deciding to do just that was the only thing that had broken this logjam of melancholy. "I think I will just go forward," she said, wiping away the black streaks under her eyes. "And I'm going to start by having a nice meal with my friend." She took Felicia's arm, gave it a firm squeeze, and led her out of the ladies' room.

38

*B*ill Seagirt knew the affair with Sissy had gone on too long. For one thing, his time with her was starting to take on too many of the rhythms of marriage. They'd finished in bed about an hour ago — and it took more and more coaxing and sweet talking to get her there in the first place — and now they were sitting on the couch, glazing over in front of the TV. At least *he* was glazing over; Sissy was keenly attentive, since this was one of her favorite soap operas. He'd have liked to have left as soon as he'd zipped up his pants, but he knew how that would have looked, so he forced himself to linger a little while.

"You want something to drink?" he asked her, getting up and heading into the kitchen.

"No, I'm fine," she said, smiling, but not taking her eyes from the screen.

He leaned into the refrigerator, looking for the beer she'd bought just for him. It was a little early for a beer, but he wasn't a diet soda kind of guy. He yanked out the beer bottle from behind her heads of lettuce and skim milk, and popped the top off. It wasn't that he didn't like Sissy, but he was already married. He wanted something different from his affairs. He wouldn't say he was proud of the affairs, but he wasn't ashamed of them, either. The way he looked at it, Bunny ought to be grateful for them. They kept him from having to leave her.

He swigged the beer looking out the kitchen window at the patch of lawn and rock garden in Sissy's backyard. He always got that same restless feeling when it was time to move on to another woman, and he'd had that feeling with Sissy for a few more weeks than he'd like. But the one he'd set his sights on next was not budging. Sure, he'd met a few women down here who weren't up for the sex, even though they'd have liked the company and attention, but they were all forgettable. This one — he'd found out her name was Angie — he was finding hard to shake, even after she'd been so hateful and vile to him. Or maybe because of that.

He rummaged in the cabinets, found a bag of chips, and sat down at the kitchen table. His last run-in with Angie was so bizarre and humiliating, it hurt him to think of it, and yet his thoughts returned to it repeatedly, the way a child longs to peek under a bandage to catalogue the horrors of a recent wound. Why had Angie taken such an instant dislike to him, so much so that she had to make up this insipid tale about being a dyke? Every once in a while, he entertained the idea that she was telling the truth, but it made so much more sense to him believe that it was just her way of telling him she wasn't interested. Besides, she just didn't look and act like a dyke, apart from being such a bitch to him, that was. And if he had an instinct about one thing in life, it was women.

Angie was a spitfire, alright, and it was funny, because that was what had attracted him to Bunny all those lifetimes ago. Odd how his tastes hadn't changed much. He'd even begun to think that maybe if he started something up with Angie, he wouldn't need to move on, that she'd be enough to hold his interest for good.

And he thought about making her happy, too. That's how he knew she was different. With the others, Sissy included, he thought about what would make them happy only so he could get what he wanted. But now he thought about what might make Angie happy just for the sake of making her happy. If his son ever got around to asking him any advice about women, that's what he'd tell him. If you find one you just want to see happy, that's how you know she's the one.

"You want me to make you a sandwich?" Sissy asked, scuffing into the kitchen in her terry cloth slippers and joining him across the table.

"Nah, I'm just picking," he said, realizing he'd polished off half the bag of chips. "I gotta get going anyway. I'm supposed to take Bunny up to the outlet stores this afternoon. She'll be wondering where I am." He thought about springing to his feet, but then he dawdled. Maybe he ought to tell Sissy right here and now that he couldn't risk it anymore.

Her eyes welled. "I'm not going to see you much

163

longer, am I? This isn't your idea of fun, is it? Watching the soaps and eating chips."

"Don't be silly, Sis," he said, startled. He reached over to cup her hand, her sad, sagging face making him lose his nerve. "We got a good thing here."

"A thing, yes."

"You know that's all I can —"

"I know, I know," Sissy said. "There's enough of us walking widowed down here. Last thing I would want is to be responsible for taking a breathing man away from his wife. I couldn't look at myself in the mirror."

"Yeah, well." He stood up. He was tired of these melancholy partings, too. Angie, he imagined, might throw him out by his butt hairs, but she wouldn't mope. She didn't seem worn down by the effort of living. He wanted someone like that. "I don't know exactly when I can get away next, Sis," he said. "My son's coming to visit."

"I understand," she said, giving him her cheek to kiss. He headed out through the living room. Her next soap opera was just coming on. He knew how that would end, too.

39

*R*ich had barely moved his finger off the buzzer when the door swung open, and Greg was standing there, in a black T-shirt and black jeans. He was a far more potent presence than Rich had allowed himself to remember.

"I was afraid you might not come," Greg said.

"Good as my word," Rich said, flustered. He wasn't used to a date — especially one so adorable — revealing how happy he was to see him. That's how Rich knew he wasn't in New York. Everyone wasn't terminally blasé.

"I'm not going to jump you in the doorway this time," Greg said.

"In that case, I'm leaving," Rich said, smiling as he walked in.

"Well, I thought I ought to play hard to get."

"Hard is good, too," Rich said, blushing at his own compulsive sex joking. It was nervousness making him do it.

"Can I get you a drink?"

"Scotch, on the rocks."

"Coming up."

Rich scanned the living room as Greg worked in the kitchen. The room was largely untouched by personality. There was a dark green leather couch, a small TV, and a glass end table. But the white walls were bare, the small window had no blinds, and there was no comfortable clutter — mail or newspapers or books — anywhere.

"Are you just moving in or just moving out?" Rich called into the kitchen.

Greg rounded the corner, carrying a drink in each hand. "A little of each, actually." He handed Rich a tumbler. "I just graduated from NYU two months ago."

Rich tried not to flinch. At least it wasn't high school.

"I was living at home before I went away to school," Greg continued, "and when I finished, I realized I couldn't move back in with my folks —"

"Really difficult to jump men in the doorway, then, eh?"

"Something like that," Greg said, grinning briefly. "But I really wasn't in any position to afford a place in New York, as much as I would have loved it. And I didn't know — still don't — what I want to do. Go to law school or work first or travel. So I just came back

166

down here and tried to figure it out. Obviously I can't stay here too long. I'm mean, no offense, but—"

"Don't apologize," Rich said, sitting on the couch next to Greg. He tried to keep their knees from touching. Even though they'd behaved so carnally at their last meeting, the span of weeks that had passed made Rich feel formal all over again. "This is no place for someone your age. I lived a full life in New York before coming here. It's made for the young, and that's who should be there. How serious are you about law school?"

"Well, it's my father who's really set on it. I don't think I'd ever want to practice law, but I like the idea of going into politics. Except that I could never do something where I had to spend my life in the closet. If I could do anything at all, it would be to try to make it as a dancer, or some kind of performer. I started a troupe at school—we called ourselves The Dancing Dicks." Rich warmed to the sound of Greg's laughter. "Me and three other guys. We all went by the name Dick. We did benefits and stuff. It was great fun. My father would kill me if he knew." Greg stirred his drink with his finger.

"Do your parents know you're gay?"

"Not yet," Greg said. "At least not that we've talked about. But I plan to tell them soon. I don't know who's going to take it harder, my mom or my dad."

"Moms have a harder time with their daughters, dads with their sons. Or at least that's my theory," Rich said. "Where do your parents live?"

"You golf?"

"Excuse me?"

"Because if you golf, you probably know my dad. He lives in your community. Bill Seagirt."

Rich, mid-sip, nearly sent a spray of scotch into Greg's face. "Bill Seagirt of *Bunny* and Bill? You're their *son?*"

"Yeah," Greg said, frowning. "So you do know them?"

Rich got up to pace. How could he tell Greg his mother was a picket-sign-waving bigot, a veritable homophobe poster girl? "Look, Greg, maybe you'd better not tell them just yet." He tossed back so big a swallow of his drink that he dribbled some down his chin.

"Why not? What's wrong? Will you sit back down, please? You're making me dizzy."

"All I mean is, why don't you decide first what you're going to do with the rest of your life." Rich perched at the end of the couch and guzzled more of his drink. He couldn't bear to even *think* now about ravaging Bunny Seagirt's progeny. "At least the next year of it. Let them adjust to that. Then you can tell them about your sexuality. That way they can't blame every decision you make on that. Forget trying to tell them you want to live in New York because it's the cultural capital of the universe. They'll think you only want to go there because it's faggot finishing school, and you'll never hear the end of it."

"God," Greg said, his head in his hand. "I didn't think of it that way. I thought if I told them they might understand why I can't live somewhere like this part of Florida."

"No, that's precisely why they'll want you to. Straighten you out. Meet a nice Southern girl."

"Yeah, you're right, I guess." Greg was looking morosely into his drink.

"Did I ruin your night?"

Greg looked up. "It's just that, I'd hoped . . . by the time I told them, I'd be bringing along the man in my life. A nice Southern gentleman . . . someone like you, actually."

Rich felt himself blush. "I don't think I fit the bill, Greg. For one thing, I'm a Yankee. And for another, a gentleman wouldn't be here if he were married like I am. Maybe I should go." Rich stood up, panic making his heart knock. It wasn't so much that he hadn't bargained for the boy thinking he was falling in love, but that he *liked* the idea of the boy thinking he was falling in love.

"I'm scaring you," Greg said. "Don't listen to me." He pulled Rich over by the hips and Rich, with his eyes closed and against his better judgment, listened to the sound of Greg unzipping his jeans.

40

When the doorbell rang, Lara's eyes flew open and she was unpleasantly surprised to see that it was already 8:35. Helen turned onto her side, tugging crankily at the sheets. Lara took that as her cue to get up. She shrugged on her striped robe and padded heavy-footed to the front door.

"I'm sorry I'm so early," Chris said. "I hardly slept the whole night so I stopped trying. I needed to talk."

Lara stepped aside and held the door open. Chris looked raccoon-eyed and gray-complexioned, prompting Lara to self-consciously smooth down her own hair. "Where's Karen?"

"Still in bed."

Lara knew that meant it was Karen that Chris needed to talk about. "Coffee then?"

"Don't pass go without it." Chris followed her into the kitchen. "Hey girl," she said to Emma, who, on hearing signs of life, emerged, swaying her backside.

"I had a rotten night, too," Lara said. "Some stupid crank caller rang the phone at two, four and six."

"You're *kid*ding," Chris said. A hushed and horrified tone in Chris's voice made Lara turn around. "The same exact thing happened to us," Chris said. "The same times, give or take a few minutes."

The two friends looked solemnly at each other. "Bunny Seagirt," they said simultaneously. Lara sank wearily into a chair.

"Do you think everybody else got the calls, too?" Lara asked.

"As long as they're listed, I bet so," Chris said.

"Let's call Angie and Ruth and ask." Lara speed dialed and put the phone on speaker so Chris could hear. It was snatched up in the middle of the first ring.

"You listen to me, you twisted, hate-mongering bigot," Angie screamed. "You petty, pea-brained fascist—"

"*Angie*, An*gie!* It's Lara! STOP!"

There was a long pause. "Lara? Why have you been calling me all night and hanging up?"

"For God's sake, I haven't. But I'm calling you now to say that both Helen and I and Chris and Karen got the same calls all night. Why don't you and Ruth come over now and we'll talk about what to do?"

"I'm through talking, Lara. Bigotry breeds in silence—I've said that my whole life. I told you last

171

time that we needed to have a stronger response when she started with her Gestapo paint chip strategy."

Lara watched Chris rolling her eyes.

"So what do you have in mind? Come over and tell us."

"No need. My plan's already in place. This little incident just sharpened my resolve. It'll be paying dividends shortly. You'll see. Gotta go." And her voice was replaced with a loud dial tone.

"Well, I guess it takes a fanatic to take on a fanatic," Chris said.

"Mmmm. Let me call the guys."

"No, don't. Not yet. This wasn't what I needed to talk to you about."

"Uh-oh," Lara said. "Let me get the coffee, then." She poured them both a cup, marveling at how its woody scent never failed to elicit a little quiver of happy anticipation, even after all these decades. Thank God some drugs were legal.

"Is it about Karen?" Lara asked, settling gingerly into a chair. Her back was balky in the morning these days.

"You've always been able to read me," Chris said, smiling. Lara feared the worst, and though she wanted to pump Chris, to get her quickly past the throat-clearing and false starts, there was no better way to get Chris to talk than to just be quiet and wait.

Chris played in the sugar bowl, scooping up and pouring back teaspoon after teaspoon of white granules. "I don't know how this could have happened. I partly moved down here for the most paranoid reasons. I figured we'd be surrounded by friends I trusted, old straight women, and widowers. Not much danger there." When she looked up, Lara could see the tears in her eyes. She squelched the urge to reach across the table and take Chris's hand, because she knew that would just make Chris lose control completely.

"I don't know if she's actually having an affair," Chris said slowly, "but I do know she's in love with another woman." Chris lifted the coffee mug with a trembling hand. "You know, I never warned her about lesbian adolescence, how you go through it whether you come out at sixteen or sixty. God, remember it? When you go from realizing you love one woman to realizing you love women in general and you want to get as many as possible into bed? And then, when you've gotten back to your senses, you realize one woman was just enough, after all, thank you very much."

"Have you said anything to her?"

"Not exactly. What is there to say? I know who the woman is — she's married, and considering how I met Karen, that shouldn't surprise me, but it does. Isn't that pathetic?"

"So you feel like you have this coming to you. That's why you're afraid to fight it."

"I don't know," Chris said, rubbing her face vigorously. "I just think I'm way past giving lovers ultimatums. I want Karen to stay with me because she *wants* to. I know I'm asking for a lot — the rest of her life. Or at least the rest of mine."

"But you have a right to ask for that. You're worth that —"

"Hey, did anybody feed Emma?" Helen called out on her way into the kitchen. The springer was running in rings around Helen's legs. Lara knew it was Helen's

173

way of announcing, from a safe distance, that she was about to intrude on their private conversation.

"I was just about to," Lara said, getting up to kiss Helen and simultaneously pull Emma's dog food bag out of the pantry. The dog was doing a four-footed tap dance.

"Good morning, Chris," Helen said.

"We've just discovered that all of us got the same series of middle-of-the-night calls," Chris said.

Lara wished Chris hadn't blurted the news to Helen this way. Everyone thought Helen, so easygoing on the surface, took these things in stride, but in fact she was a brooder, and she would take this very hard. And Chris, threatened by the loss of Karen on top of all this, was on the brink of full-scale personal meltdown. Lara studied both their worried faces, and felt a clutch of anxiety in own chest.

"Look, no more dwelling on this," Lara said. "We'll just unplug our phones at night for a few weeks till Bunny gets tired of her little game. And she will. Until then, we're going to do what we came down here to do — enjoy our lives, and our well-deserved retirement." She reached across the kitchen table and patted Chris's cheek. They'd have to finish their conversation later. "Got it?"

"Well," Chris said, "okay. But I'm secretly hoping, for a change, that Angie is really as pissed as she sounded."

41

*K*aren finally got up the nerve to push open the gallery door, the new painting under her arm. Georgia was feather-dusting a sculpture and broke into a slow smile when she turned and saw her. Karen felt herself blush.

"I was beginning to be afraid I wouldn't ever see you again," Georgia said.

"Commerce must go on," Karen said, straining for light-heartedness. She held the canvas out, wrapped in brown paper, to spare herself Georgia's scrutiny of it. "Birdbath, part two, I guess you could say."

"Terrific." Georgia reached for it without taking her eyes off Karen. "No one else is in the store right now — let's keep it that way, shall we?" She walked behind Karen, locked the door, and hung up the "Be back shortly" sign. "Come into the office and let's have a good look at the painting — and you."

"Georgia, I didn't come here to —"

"Oh, hush and give your friend five minutes." Georgia led the way into the back, the shimmering, burgundy material of her pantsuit rippling behind her.

Karen stayed frozen in place. The right thing to do, she knew, was to unlock the front door and leave. Because she wasn't sure she could trust herself to resist Georgia. She wanted to keep the promise she'd made herself to end this. Because what was it, really? Just lust, all covered over with the little thrills and tricks we play on ourselves when we tell ourselves we're in love. Chris was a far better companion, a far better lifemate, and it didn't hurt to apply some common sense when it came to long-term love. And yet, when Karen moved her feet, she found herself heading into the back after Georgia.

Karen stopped at the threshold; Georgia was leaning against the desk, waiting. "I'm not —"

"Don't be like this," Georgia said, more forcefully than Karen had expected. She had expected coy. "For God's sake, come in and just let's talk." Georgia crossed the room, took Karen by the wrist, and led her over to the paisley couch. "I've tried not to, but I've missed you," she whispered, reaching out for Karen's cheek slowly, as if she thought contact with it might hurt and therefore required caution.

Karen steeled herself against the flutter Georgia's touch roused. "Georgia, don't do this. I'm not going to do this."

"But it's already done. I've wanted to call you a couple of thousand times a day. I know I said we shouldn't go on, too, but I didn't count on —"

176

"Stop it," Karen said, bounding to her feet. "I'm not going to be your extracurricular entertainment, your diversion when Hank isn't whisking you off on some vacation or business here is a little slow. I'm not going to hurt Chris. I'm not going to let you screw up our lives until you decide you're bored." *Leave now,* Karen told herself, but she saw there were tears in Georgia's eyes, and her resolve crumbled.

"You're punishing me for telling you about that other woman a hundred years ago. But that has nothing to do with what I'm feeling now." Georgia approached, took both of Karen's hands, and kissed her. Karen didn't struggle; she'd replayed their kisses in her head countless times, and had tried to summon exactly these sensations, of Georgia's lips and tongue, warm and pliant, the pressure of her large breasts against her as she drew closer in. She allowed herself to savor it, willed herself to memorize it, then broke away.

"Georgia, at my age, you are a lovely detour I don't have time to take anymore."

"And at my age, you're a detour I can't afford *not* to take." Georgia's hands were on Karen's shoulders, slipping down her back.

Karen felt the danger in the moment. All she'd need to do was reach out and they'd be making love again. The moment was just a few seconds into the future; it was fully formed, she knew, in both their imaginations.

"No — it costs you nothing," Karen said, backing out of Georgia's embrace. "You want me to shoulder all the risk."

"If you want me to, I'll leave Hank."

"Don't toy with me." Karen felt a wave of anger

warm her cheeks. "Every unhappy marriage does not spawn a lesbian. If it did, we wouldn't be a minority anymore."

"Is that it? I'm not a registered lesbian, so you can't take me seriously? It wasn't so long ago that you yourself were some man's wife."

"You said yourself you still love Hank."

Georgia sank onto the couch. "I do, in our way. He loved making money, I loved spending it, and we enjoyed together the things I spent it on. The summer house. The European vacations. The art. That's no small thing, to have that in common. People stay married who share a lot less." Georgia covered her mouth and shut her eyes. Karen prayed Georgia wouldn't cry; it would level whatever willpower she had left. "But that doesn't mean that I can't want someone else now. In a different way. Just because, all those years ago, I didn't love Marisa" — hearing the woman's name gave Karen a little jolt — "doesn't mean I can't love you now. Do I have to have loved any woman I slept with, and not loved my husband, for you to believe I can love you now? Maybe I *was* in love with Marisa back then and told myself I wasn't — would that make you feel better?"

"That's the difference between you and me," Karen said. "You think you can choose what you feel. Or you only feel what you choose. It suits you right now to think you're in love. It's a little more interesting, a little more arty, if that person is another woman."

"For *God's* sake, Karen, give me more credit than that." Georgia's voice was shaking. "Just because I'm not having some sexual identity crisis of the kind you would consider appropriate, don't accuse me of not knowing what I'm getting into. Isn't it enough of a

178

crisis to be married to one person if you're in love with another? Isn't that the main thing?"

"Oh, so now you're too sophisticated to be upset that maybe you've been a closet case for the last twenty-five years?" Karen said. She felt reckless with righteousness. "How many of the women artists you've been 'nurturing' have you really been in love with from afar? Did I seduce you all on my own, or weren't you really letting me know you were ready? How many straight women were you signaling to over the years, and then were both relieved and disappointed when they didn't respond?"

Georgia straightened up on the couch. Karen saw that she had insulted her profoundly enough that there might not be a way to repair it. She felt, from the way Georgia set her shoulders, that she was being dismissed, in something of a permanent way. It was one of those surreal moments, she registered, when the present slips between your fingers and you're as powerless to grasp at it as you are at time itself.

"You're telling your own story, now, aren't you, Karen? I didn't spend *my* life living one thing and wanting another. I'm sorry for you — genuinely — if you waited so many years to have what you wanted. But I don't regret my life with Hank. And I wouldn't leave him now, either, if it weren't important to you. But just because you feel obligated to Chris for saving you from a lifetime of emptiness, don't pretend to me that what happened between us means nothing to you. Don't make me out in your own mind as some kind of evil dilettante so you can live with your own choices."

My God, how did they so quickly get to this place where lovers said such hateful things to each other? Karen felt the blackness of regret descend; if only she could turn and flee quickly enough, maybe she could outrun it.

"Karen," Georgia called after her. "When are you going to start living the life you want? None of us has all the time in the world, anymore."

Karen kept moving, through the gallery and toward the door. She told herself it was better this way. It just was.

42

Angie watched Rich as he swam across his backyard pool, his knife-sharp strokes slicing through the water's surface with hardly a splash. It was impossible not to admire the streamlined efficiency of his body; it was not even beyond her imagination to find him desirable. It was just that, in her whole life, she had never fallen in love with a man, never worked up anything past a chummy camaraderie, and even at that, it was mostly with gay men. It was as if men were a different species altogether, one that, like, say, cheetahs, she could admire on its own terms, but would consider unnatural to mate with.

She watched him towel off vigorously, sending the graying hairs on his legs sticking up in all the wrong directions. He plopped onto the chaise lounge next to her, and smoothed his hair back from his forehead into a slick, silver plane. "Ah," he said, smiling up into the morning sun. "This is the life."

"Deep," Angie said, with exaggerated sourness. They had a kind of banter, she and Rich, that they had locked into early and neither could figure out how to escape. He played to the hilt the guilt-free hedonist, she — far more than she felt — the tortured intellectual. In reality, they both knew, Rich was every bit as smart and concerned about the world as Angie was, and gave plenty of money to gay causes; he just didn't wear any of it on his sleeve the way she felt compelled to. And her own indulgences she sometimes felt driven to hide from him, so he didn't tease her the way she knew he would.

"So, Ang, to what do I owe the pleasure of this visit?" Rich asked, reaching for his sunglasses as much, she suspected, to complete the look as to shield his eyes.

"I need you to handle something for me. Something that needs to be handled man-to-man."

"I'm interested already."

"Not *that* kind of man-to-man," Angie reprimanded.

"Ah. I forget there's any other kind."

"It's about Bunny Seagirt, the one-woman noise pollution hazard."

Rich dropped his smile and scowled into the pool. "No. Whatever it is, the answer is no. Besides, what's man-to-man about that? Are you telling me she's secretly a drag queen?"

"Just hear me out, will you?" Angie took the photos out of the envelope she was carrying and handed them over.

"What am I looking at?" Rich asked, flipping

through them. "This is a bunch of pictures of a guy walking in and out of a house."

"Not just any guy. Bunny Seagirt's husband, Bill. And the house — see the number on the door — isn't his house. It's obviously the house of his little side dish."

Rich pushed his sunglasses down his nose and looked at Angie over the top of them. "Are you talking blackmail?"

"You were always a quick study, Rich. I knew I could count on you."

"Wait a minute — I didn't agree to anything. How'd you get these pictures anyway?"

"Surveillance," Angie said breezily. "See, the problem is, I can't confront him, because he's been hitting on me since we moved down here, and we had a little, uh, incident in the clubhouse pool, and it could appear I simply am out to get him."

"An incident?"

"It's not important. The point is, I'm sullied. I can't be the one to accuse him."

"And I can? Forget it, Angie."

"Rich, *please*. It's easy. All you have to do is show Bill the pictures and say we won't tell dear Bunny about them if he just convinces her to back the hell off her homophobic harassment. I don't consider that blackmail. I consider that making her do the right thing, since she hasn't got the decency to do it herself. Rich, we are under attack, here, don't forget."

"I am not going to stoop to that level. No way, Ang. You've got the wrong man." He handed the photos back.

"Rich, listen to reason. Nothing, I mean *nothing*, is going to make Bunny simply see the light and welcome us to the neighborhood. Reasoning with her is not an option. First the petition, now the phone calls — it's clearly going to escalate. So we either live with increasing antagonism or we move out."

"Or she moves out," Rich said.

"You know she'd die before she'd do that, just on principle. My way, we shift the pressure back where it belongs — onto Bunny Seagirt."

"And did you ever consider the possibility that Bill Seagirt laughs at the pictures, says they prove nothing, and tells me to shove them up my very attractive and well-toned ass?"

"Bill Seagirt would never say you had a very attractive and well-toned ass."

"So clearly we can't rely on his judgment."

"It's worth a try, isn't it?"

"No. No, it's not," Rich said, folding his arms over his chest. "Because I still don't want to be associated with those kinds of tactics. And I don't want Bill Seagirt to think that's what our community is about. We'd be asking him not to make an issue of our private lives by making an issue of *his* private life!"

"Only because his butt-head wife made an issue of it first."

"No way, Ang. And don't think of asking Rudy, either. He's catering an event for her."

"What! Are you serious? He's doing business with the enemy — are you both nuts?"

Rich sighed heavily. "Ang, it's a different strategy. It's called acting like a normal member of the community, and maybe people will start treating us like normal members of the community."

"Rich, you aren't that naive, and I know it. You volunteered for the Anti-Violence Project for years, for Christ's sake. People like Bunny don't care if you press your slacks with a crease as good as her husband's. She doesn't want you to have the same right to breathe the air she does — just *because*."

Rich took off his sunglasses and massaged the bridge of his nose for a long moment. "Ang, look," he said, "I can't do this. I can't do it because . . . because I'm fucking the Seagirts's son, okay? That's why." He put his sunglasses back on and lay very still on the lounge chair, his arms stiff at his sides.

Angie just stared. She had no idea that the Seagirts had a son, let alone a queer one, let alone a queer one in the neighborhood who'd happened to meet up with Rich with his fly undone. But she didn't doubt for a second that Rich was telling the truth. He didn't joke about stuff like that. "You stinking, low-life son of a bitch," she spat out finally.

"Believe me, I called myself worse when I found out who he was."

"You mean," Angie said, "you didn't even know who he was before you had your hands down his pants?"

"It's a kind of protocol."

"This is unbelievable! This is just grand!" Angie got up and began to stomp in circles around their chairs. "I've got a psychopathic homophobe trying to run all of us out of town, and I've got two friends, one of whom is making her cucumber finger-sandwiches and the other one of whom is sucking her son's dick. And then you all tell me *I'm* acting like an insane person!"

"Angie, sit down and shut up."

For no other reason than abject depression, she obeyed.

"Rudy and I had a fight one night. I went to the nearest bar in a rage. He turned out to be a sweet kid. I felt kind of . . . paternal."

"Oh, that's cute. Who's your role model? Catholic priests?"

Rich yanked off his sunglasses again. "And Rudy is running a business. He can't discriminate against customers. Even when she's a heterosexist hothead with a beige fetish."

Angie curled into a fetal position on the lounge chair and began to moan. "So now what do we do?"

"I don't know. Something else. Slaughter small animals. Wait for a miracle."

"Do you see all the trouble the world comes to because men can't keep their pants zipped?"

"Take my advice, Ang. Don't run a campaign on that platform. You've got gay men, straight men and straight women as the pro-penis vote."

"Just goes to show you. Majority rules is a stupid idea."

43

*L*ara walked slowly down the block, the sight of their house in the near distance flooding her with relief. She had set out a mere half hour ago on an early morning walk — Helen had stayed behind to tend the garden — but the heat had descended quickly, pressing down on all sides like a force field, making the air as hard to breathe as molasses. Her whole body was bathed in a film of perspiration. Why hadn't anyone warned them that this part of Florida was virtually uninhabitable in late July? She marveled that the trees didn't slump over like melted rubber, and began to fantasize about how good the cool, air-conditioned air of the house would feel against her skin.

As she neared the house, she heard, unmistakably,

Emma's howling. It was piercing, the pitch of ancient heartbreak of the most inconsolable kind, and she had heard it from Emma only rarely. Full of dread, Lara broke into a jerky jog, pushing her leaden legs to pump against the heat, ignoring the labored sound of her own breathing. She ran clumsily up the walk and lunged for the front door, but Emma's baying was around back, she determined, and she hurried down the front steps to round the corner. Where was Helen that she was letting Emma carry on so? "Helen! *Hel*en! *Helen!* " Lara shouted, her voice hoarse and shaky. Emma bounded forward, her tongue lolling out the side of her mouth, and turned and charged back into the yard.

And then Lara saw the source of Emma's distress: Helen, on her knees, was crumpled over in the flower bed, like a child who, exhausted from play, merely fell asleep amidst her toys. One hand, in a muddy canvas garden glove, was still circled loosely around the handle of the watering can. Emma was running in circles, barking in hysterical spasms, and Lara watched as the sun imploded into a dark, angry speck, and the world was shuttered in darkness.

44

*S*issy Armonk would not have been able to imagine the circumstances under which she would ever have arrived at Billy Seagirt's front door to ring the bell. Secrecy had informed their every move, concealment and camouflage had been the terms of their affair. But here she was, in broad daylight, about to destroy all their efforts in one simple, destructive act.

A thin woman with teased, frosted hair opened the door, her face already gathered into annoyed impatience. She was not expecting anyone — that was clear from the white and violet lounging robe she clutched around herself — and she made no attempt to hide her displeasure.

"You must be Bunny Seagirt," Sissy said, smiling the

smile of her Southern manners. "I'm here to talk to you about your husband. May I come in?"

"What about my husband? Who are you? What do you want?" Bunny asked, her frown deepening, making her whole face seem to fold inward like an accordion. Sissy knew Billy was off at a golf game this morning so there was no danger of his being home. She pressed on with her mission in confidence.

"Well, I'm Sissy Armonk, but I can't tell you the rest from out here," Sissy said, as sweet as she could muster. She fanned herself with her scented handkerchief and made a show of squinting painfully up into the sun. "And once you understand, you'll be grateful for having invited me in."

Bunny stepped back a grudging few feet, just enough for Sissy to squeeze through into the foyer. "What is it?" Bunny demanded when the door hissed shut.

"*Wellll,*" Sissy said, drawing the word out to buy herself some time. She had lain awake for nights rehearsing this revenge, but now that the moment had arrived, she found herself reluctant, a stranger to the very motives that drove her here. Because, after all, what did Bunny Seagirt have to do with Sissy's anger? Destroying this marriage was bound to hurt Bunny more than Billy. And none of it, she knew now, would bring Billy back to her anyway.

"What is it, already, you silly old woman?" Bunny demanded.

That was enough to revive Sissy. "I'm your husband's mistress," Sissy blurted. "Or I was until very recently, when he got tired of me and moved on to the next conquest. It just offended my sense of decency to think that three-quarters of the community knows your husband is as horny as a morning rooster and faithful as a cockroach, and everyone knows it but you."

Bunny's lips and eyes twitched oddly, as if her face were rigged with springs that, long compressed, were suddenly released. This went on for several minutes; Sissy didn't know whether to laugh or call an ambulance.

"Get out of my house, you conniving whore," Bunny said. "I don't know what you expect with your filthy lies, but whatever it is, you won't get it from me." Bunny threw the front door open with a rigid arm.

"Oh, I don't blame you. I'd do the same thing, honey," Sissy said amiably. "You can call me a whore, I guess, but I don't want you to call me a liar. How else would I know that Billy's pecker curves a little to the left when it's happy, dear? Or has it been so long for the two of you that you don't remember?"

"Get out! Get *out!* This instant! Before I call the police!" Bunny shrieked, the loose skin of her neck quivering conspicuously with the effort. Sissy thought herself in far better shape, personally, and the observation gave her courage.

"Well, I don't know what they could do for you, *Mrs.* Seagirt," Sissy said. "It isn't a crime in the state of Florida to tell the truth." It was a good parting shot, Sissy complimented herself as she strolled down the walk. And it made her so happy, she hardly flinched as Bunny slammed the door so hard she could hear the windows rattle.

45

*H*elen opened her eyes to wall-to-wall whiteness, and in her woozy semiconsciousness, she thought it must be snow. Cold, bracing snow, the kind she knew up north, the kind that made your toes burn and your nose sting, the kind that floated feather-light to the ground and yet piled as heavy and solid as sand.

"Helen? Helen, can you hear us?"

It wasn't snow then at all. As she feared, it was a hospital room, and all that she prayed she had been dreaming must be true. Chris and Karen, and Angie and Ruth were standing at her bedside on her left, and Rich and Rudy were seated on the right. They all looked as sick and terrified as she felt. They would be of no help, but they were apparently all she had.

"Where's Lara?"

Chris's chin dimpled, and her bottom lip jutted wetly forward. She squeezed Helen's hand. Helen turned to the guys.

"Will one of you tell me?" Helen watched their grave faces and wondered at her own cruelty at making them repeat the news, because she recalled now every terrible thing they had told her earlier. After that, she recalled a doctor had rushed forward with a needle. But still, she held out hope that maybe the memory was some kind of sedative-induced nightmare.

"Oh, darling," Rudy said, reaching across her waist to tuck the sheets in around her more tightly. Next to him, Rich looked chastened, like a soldier who was supposed to have returned home triumphant, and who instead has been badly trounced. "She's gone," Rudy said. "Do you remember anything?" He was watching her, his eyebrows arched with hope. "She found you in the garden, passed out. You had heat stroke, a little dehydration, but she must have taken you for dead. It was such a shock, she went into cardiac arrest. Massive. They never revived her."

It was ridiculous information, incomprehensible, grotesque and impossible. She had thought so before, and had gotten hysterical, which was why the doctor, with his sedative, had been called. The last thing she remembered was his face turning wavy, and then swirling out of sight, like something going down a drain. They were all looking at their feet now, shuffling, sniffling, all as useless as children. If Lara were here, she'd be the strong one for them all. "She never could take a scare well," Helen said, giving herself over to a macabre giggle. None of them joined her, their faces taut with shock. She knew they thought her mad, mad with grief, and maybe she was. What choice did she have? Was sanity any kind of solace? "Did it just happen today? Is it still the same day?" she asked, a new panic gripping her.

"Yes. It's night. Of the same day," Ruth said.

"Has anyone taken care of Emma?" Helen asked, angrily, because she knew none of them had. Chris looked across the bed at the guys, who shrugged and stammered. Emma was the last one to see Lara alive. She had tried to save them both, no doubt, and Helen knew the spaniel was feeling something of the same shock she herself was feeling now.

"We didn't think of her, Helen," Chris said. "There was so much else to do."

Helen heard the wounded sound in Chris's voice and had no stomach for it. "For God's sake, do you want me to go home to find my dog dead, too?"

She couldn't bear to look at any of them, though she felt all their eyes on her. She had no energy to explain, to describe how utterly alone in the universe she felt, how stripped bare and abandoned, how impossible the task of going on without Lara was.

"I'll go see to Emma," Rich said, jumping up. "I've got a copy of your key." He leaned down and kissed Helen's forehead before quickly ducking out.

Helen scanned her mind to decide what needed doing next. "Chris, can you —"

"I've got the will. Everything's in motion, Helen. Don't worry about those details. The funeral is the day after next."

The funeral. Lara's funeral. The most terrible thing in her life that she had to face, and Lara wasn't there to help her through it. All she had left were these friends, friends who, once warmed by the vantage of being part of a couple, she thought sweet and fond and true. Now they floated without context, without value, useless and mocking, pallid, powerless, pointless.

"Leave me alone, now," Helen said. "I can't bear company," she managed, straining to conceal the full measure of her contempt and rage. It wasn't their faults, after all, that all of them put together and multiplied by ten, could not make up for even a fraction of Lara's love.

46

*B*unny watched happily as Greg polished off his food, category by category, as he had done ever since he was a child. First the potatoes, then the peas, then the sliced pot roast.

"I thought you weren't going to cook, ma," Greg said, wiping his mouth with his napkin.

"I don't see you complaining. You cleaned your plate," she said.

"All I mean is, I thought you were going to give yourself a break."

"I couldn't find a good caterer in town," she said, folding her arms.

"What about that Rudy's place?" Bill asked. "I've heard only good things —"

"I canceled the order. It's a dirty place," Bunny said

ominously. She gave her husband the most withering look she could muster. Sissy Armonk had visited just yesterday, and the only reason Bunny had put off a showdown with her husband was that she hadn't wanted to ruin this rare and overdue visit from their son. But if Sissy's story were true — and Bunny had no doubts at all that she'd be able to determine that from Bill's reaction, even if it was a flat-out denial — peace on earth as he had known it was about to end for him forever.

She smiled back at her son. "Greg, you are just looking so handsome. All muscled like you are. Of course, I'd rather see you wear something besides those tight jeans once in a while. But I've been so sure you're home to tell us you've got a girl."

"Wow," Greg said, pushing away from the table. "That's a record, ma. We didn't even make it to dessert before you brought the subject up."

"The boy's right, Bunny," Bill said. "Stop badgering him. He's in his prime. He's probably got so many girls he can't keep track. Quit bugging him to settle down. A man's got most of his life to be married to one woman. Let him enjoy himself while he can."

Bunny fantasized a scene in vivid color: she was stabbing her husband through the heart with her soiled dinner knife. She managed to restrain herself from acting on it only by promising herself that there was plenty of time for that later. She would not let him spoil the little time she had with Greg. "Greg, honey, I just want you to be happy."

"That's great, ma. I'm glad to hear you say that."

She did not like something about his tone of voice. He was mocking her.

"Ma, dad, look, I've got something to tell you. But

it's not to ask your approval or your permission. It's just a fact about my life, about me." As he spoke, he cracked his knuckles — index, middle, ring — and Bunny winced with each one. "It's not even especially new. And it's not going to change. So you might as well know it." He paused and looked from one to the other of them, gripping the edge of the table like a swimmer about to push off at the pool's edge. "I'm gay."

The scream that swirled above all their heads — as needle-sharp as a tea kettle long past its first shrill note — surprised even Bunny, even as she was aware it was coming from her own throat. And it kept coming in fresh waves, powered by the strength of her own outrage. She was on her feet, her chair kicked away from behind her, her chin pointed at the ceiling, before she felt Bill slap her.

"Bunny. For God's sake. Get a grip."

She eyed him with all the contempt she usually mustered for a bug she was about to stomp. "You yellow-bellied, festered piece of hog's manure. You scheming, cheating, lying lowlife rat's asshole, you have no right to lay a hand on me."

"Bunny!" Bill asked, his face gone pasty. "What in God's name are you —"

"I had a visit from your paramour yesterday, who saw fit to tell me, by way of establishing her credibility, all about the curvature of your pecker —"

"*What! ?*"

"Guys, hey," Greg shouted. "Knock it off! Truce! Cool it! What the hell is going on? We're supposed to be arguing about *me,* here!"

"Shut up," Bunny and Bill shouted at Greg in unison.

Then Bunny turned on Bill again. "Don't you dare talk to my son that way!"

"Fine! He's *your* son, all right," Bill boomed. "Because *I* sure didn't turn him into a faggot." Bill's face was bright red and Bunny hoped his head would explode right in front of her eyes.

"Don't call me a faggot, you son of a bitch," Greg said, on his feet, his hands balled into fists at his side.

"No — you're right, son. You've got the right idea," Bill shouted, spit flying from his lips. "I don't blame you. Women are psychotic. They're insane. They're not worth the trouble. If I could get hard for guys, I'd do it, too, I swear! At least you can reason with a man."

"You are the most revolting human being on the planet!" Bunny screamed, clapping her hands to her ears.

"I'm not gay because I hate women, dad. *You* hate women. Most womanizers do."

"Oh, so you've known all along about your father and haven't seen fit to tell me?" Bunny shrieked at her son.

"Oh, so now you're an expert in heterosexual behavior, son?" Bill sneered at Greg.

"Stop picking on him!" Bunny and Bill yelled at each other.

"This is *your* fault," Bill said. "He's a three-dollar bill because he saw what hell it is to be married to a woman like you."

"He's sick because of *you,* because you are the most pathetic role model of a husband in the history of civilized man!" Bunny smashed her dinner plate to the floor, feeling her rage expand as the shattered pieces flew to all ends of the kitchen.

"Hey, this is all too poignant for me," Greg said,

backing out of the room. "Call me when you guys figure out who you hate most, and we can talk more about this then."

As the door slammed behind him, Bunny glared at her husband and heard him bellow the very same words she hurled at him: "*Now* look what you've done!"

47

*C*hris cursed the blazingly hot day; it was obscene weather for a funeral. The parched grass crackled under their feet, and the whole procession of them — she and Karen, Rich and Rudy, each supporting Helen with an arm, Angie and Ruth, Felicia and Ted — fought the pull of heat and grief and stood, each unsteady in her own way, at the open grave.

Lara's will had called for a woman minister, one who would officiate openly for a lesbian couple, and Chris had to call as far away as two hundred miles to get a Unitarian minister to come. She was a handsome, dignified woman, with thick blond hair brushed away from her face. She stood at the head of the grave, her white robes motionless in the windless day, and read:

"And Ruth said unto Naomi, Intreat me not to leave thee, or to return from following after thee: for whither thou goest, I will go; and where thou lodgest, I will lodge: thy people shall be my people, and thy God my God:

"Where thou diest, will I die, and there will I be buried: the Lord do so to me, and more also, if ought but death part thee and me."

Helen stepped close and began to toss irises — thirty-five of them, Chris knew, one for each year they had been together — down to the bottom of the grave. Chris silently counted as Helen's hand reached out over and over, releasing a flower, and Chris felt each falling like a stone against her heart. Seventeen, eighteen, nineteen . . . Chris was crying openly now, the tears sticking as they struggled down her perspired face . . . twenty, twenty-one, twenty-two. Karen, beside her, tightened her grip around her waist, and Chris realized she was about to faint. Then she saw Helen drop to her knees and sag forward, her forehead nearly touching the grass. They all rushed toward her, but the minister held them off with one swooping, white-robed arm, and sheltered Helen as if she were a shivering child. Soon Helen resumed her slow-motion work over the grave, releasing the irises like purple wands . . . thirty-three, thirty-four, thirty-five, till none were left.

They dispersed silently, all to their cars, except Felicia and Ted, to make the two-hour drive to the beach, where the plan was to find as deserted a spot as possible to simply sit and talk. The arrangement was for Helen to go in Rich and Rudy's car, which Chris was angry about on several counts. She, after all, had known Lara longer than any of them, even longer than

Helen. Love was not measured in years, Chris knew, but then neither should it be measured by flesh. She and Lara were not lovers — although some echo of their brief affair forty years ago was always a mild current in their bond — but they were friends, true friends, as rare a thing as true marriage. She was bitter about being treated like just one of the gang. And she was bitter about Helen being given the center stage for mourning, when she herself felt Lara's death as her own particular and important loss. Mixed in with all of it was disgust at her own pettiness, and yet there it was, as stubborn as in a two-year-old.

Karen reached over and squeezed Chris's thigh. Chris eased her grip on the steering wheel; she hadn't realized how hard she'd been holding on to it.

"I can sense how I'm no comfort to you at all today," Karen said, quietly, as if they were still in church. "That's a whole other layer of grief I have, because I know what you're doing. You're thinking our relationship can't match Helen and Lara's, and you're thinking our friendship can't match yours and Lara's."

A scalding blush raced up Chris's face. She was embarrassed at how transparent she was and angry at having her self-pity discovered. She longed for exile and revenge; not for a minute had she dismissed her suspicions about Karen and the woman in the portrait. "After this is over, I want you to move out," Chris said. "I deserve someone who loves me," she said, pausing, "beyond the shadow of a doubt."

Karen lifted her hand away. "This is not a good time to make decisions, Chris."

"I made it before. I just didn't have the courage to tell you."

Out of the corner of her eye, Chris saw Karen start

203

to cry, new tears to join the graveside ones that hadn't dried yet. But as much as Chris wanted to, she didn't turn to look at Karen, to comfort or forgive. Lara was dead, and she blamed everyone for it.

48

I guess I wanted to tell you I'm taking your advice," Greg said. They were back in Greg's apartment and Greg was sitting on the floor. Rich, on the couch, was hoping he'd stay put there. When Greg phoned to say he needed to talk, Rich had tried to get him to meet in a public place, but Greg protested. "We don't have to fool around if you don't want to," Greg had said. But Greg didn't understand that for Rich, wanting to was not the point.

"Which part?" Rich asked.

"About going to New York. Although I wish I could say I decided it all on my own. I got a call from a guy in my graduating class who needed a third person in a share in Chelsea. So that certainly makes it affordable. I figure I can get a waiter's job till I figure out what I want to do. And one thing's for sure—I can't stay here. Every day, my parents alternate coming over. And then they each complain to me about the other, and finish off by trying to save me from a life of sin. My mother refuses to believe I'm queer, but she lectures about spilling seed, anyway. And my father! It's the first time in his life he ever brought me a package of condoms and told me to use them. He never did it when he thought I was sleeping with girls. This time he said, 'Bring your own. You know how men are.' I thought I'd die."

Rich laughed. "But how do you think your mother is really taking it?" Rich knew, far more than Greg did yet, how angry a woman Bunny Seagirt was, and he feared that somehow she'd take that rage out further on Paxton Court.

"She's hurting. She feels like her husband betrayed her with other women, and her son with other men."

"Mmmm . . . ouch."

Greg untied his sneaker, carefully tugged the lace tighter, and retied it slowly, as if the bow were on a package and not his foot. "Um, I really, I wanted to see you because I don't want this to be good-bye."

Rich swallowed; he found himself on the brink of tears at the slightest provocation since Lara's death, provocation far less significant than Greg's leaving. He focused hard now on keeping his composure. "I can't promise you I'll visit."

Greg caught his bottom lip between his teeth. "Well, I actually was going to go as far as asking you if you'd move back up to New York."

Rich had left Manhattan in large part to outrun death, and yet death had found him, anyway, and moved in next door. The day they all sat on the beach after Lara's funeral, Rudy broke down in tears, burying his face in his hands. He was going to quit the catering business, he said. He had been wrong, he said; love can be, *ought* to be a full-time occupation after all. He was only sorry he hadn't figured that out sooner in his life. Rich felt as though something had broken open between them in that moment, revealed an ever deeper bond and Rich felt it was something miraculous. He considered it a gift from Lara's passing, something she knew about and intended, from wherever she newly was on the other side of life as they knew it.

"Bad timing, counselor," Rich said to Greg now. Years of loving Rudy had marked him in an indelible way, the way a river carves into stone. "It looks like I'm retired. But if I were a younger man, you'd have had yourself a roommate."

Greg smiled; it was a smile, Rich thought, to show that he would concede gracefully. Rich wondered if the boy knew what he was really thinking: that if he really were a younger man once more, it would be Rudy he'd hope to meet all over again, and be as lucky as they had been.

49

*N*o one had asked her to, and certainly no one expected her to, but Felicia was bound and determined to visit Helen every day. She saw that all Helen's friends in Paxton Court were keeping vigil round the clock, coming and going in pairs or solo. Felicia went every day at four o'clock, the time Helen used to round the corner with Emma, a walk she no longer took. In fact, Helen ventured out less and less each day, and Felicia started bringing over milk and eggs and juice, things she thought would be nourishing, even if Helen didn't have the spirit to make a simple meal.

Today Felicia carried with her a big bowl of her homemade spaghetti and meatballs, the same dish she had prepared the one and only time she and Ted had

had Helen and Lara over. Every day Felicia regretted that that had been their only meal together, regretted it because she would have liked to have known better the person Helen had loved so long and so well, would have liked to have been able to pool her memories in order to be more of a comfort to Helen. She worried that maybe the association with the meal would depress Helen further, but she decided to gamble that it might be a comfort.

Felicia stood outside the front door and rang the bell for a long time. The hot spell had broken slightly, and she was grateful. She had learned not to get impatient waiting for Helen to answer the door; often she had been asleep, or just lying in bed staring at the ceiling, and it took her a while to rouse herself. The bowl of spaghetti was getting heavier and clammier in her arms.

But this was entirely too long, Felicia decided. She put the bowl down on the step and tried to figure out how to stanch her growing panic. Should she call the police? Break a window? Instead, all she did was go up and down the three steps, rubbing her upper arms in indecision.

Then she caught a whiff of it: the stink of car exhaust. She clambered down the walkway to the garage, and saw the fumes puffing steadily out from under the closed garage door. With a strength Felicia no longer knew she had, she gripped the door handle and threw it high over her head. The burst of exhaust sent her choking and reeling backward, and when it cleared some, she saw Helen, slumped, in the front seat of her car.

"Lord in heaven! Mercy, mercy, mercy!" Felicia yelled, yanking open the car door, reaching over to turn the car off, and tugging Helen by one arm. "Oh, my God!" Felicia screamed, as Helen slid off the seat and fell full up against Felicia, nearly knocking her over. Felicia wrestled Helen to a sitting position, Helen's head lolling all the while, and dragged her, by the armpits, out to the driveway and fresh air. Felicia felt the muscles in her neck and shoulders burning with pain and purpose; she was coughing so hard her throat felt bruised.

Instinctively, she began pounding Helen on the back. She made what she feared were ineffectual attempts to breathe into Helen's mouth, cursing, crying and praying in some combination incomprehensible even to herself.

Suddenly, Helen coughed. It was a lame effort at first, but then it gathered strength, till she was hacking her cheeks bright red, wracking herself onto all fours, breathing in great gulps of good, life-giving air. Felicia watched her, sobbing, till she found her own voice.

"Don't you *ever* try a trick like that again," Felicia commanded, grabbing for Helen's shoulders and pulling her close.

"Oh, Felicia, I'm sorry." Helen's voice dissolved into coughs again.

"I can't give you a reason to live, child," Felicia said. "Life is the only reason to live. That's all. That's all there is to it."

And the two women sat on the hot concrete, rocking in each other's arms, till all the smoke had cleared.

50

*T*he last thing I want is for you to feel pressured," Georgia was saying across the small restaurant table. Karen had, with a mix of dread and excitement, agreed to meet Georgia, who said she had important news she wanted to deliver in person. To Karen's eyes, Georgia, in a vibrant royal blue tunic and slacks, seemed appealingly untouched by death at a time when everyone else — especially Chris — seemed less alive since Lara's funeral.

"What kind of pressure? What do you mean?" Karen asked. She poked at the home fries on her plate and glanced nervously around to see if anyone appeared to be within earshot. Social paranoia was a habit she had developed ever since she began living as a lesbian, and she hadn't yet been able to shake it. She imagined the woman over at the corner table, for instance, the one with the sky-blue hair and the pink sweatsuit, leaping to her feet and shrieking, with her mouth wide open, if she were told about the ways she and Georgia had touched each other.

Karen turned back to find Georgia looking intently at her. "I'm leaving Hank."

Karen felt her guts knot up. She frowned down into her plate, traced patterns in the green tablecloth, anything to keep from meeting Georgia's eyes. What was she afraid Georgia might see? What would be the worst thing? Triumph? Relief? Lust? Panic? Because Karen felt all those things at once, each releasing its own poison into her system. She felt an unexpected pang of sorrow for Hank since he, too, was being sent away. If she had thought of Georgia at all in the weeks since Chris had asked her to leave, it was mostly to hate her for having been the only one spared the repercussions of their passion. "I wish you had talked to me before you made any decision," Karen said.

"No, that's exactly my point. I'm not leaving him for you," Georgia said, smiling in a self-satisfied way as if, Karen thought, a trap she had set proved effective. "I'm just leaving *him*."

"What will you do?" Divorce, Karen hadn't forgotten, was never easy, even when you didn't love the person anymore. At least Georgia didn't have kids to make the wrenching apart even more painful.

"Well, I'll keep the gallery, of course. Hank — I don't know — he'll probably move away. But in a funny way, I hope he doesn't. I consider him a friend. I think that's all we have been for a long time."

Karen blushed; even her eyelids grew hot. She saw in Georgia's sly smile the implication: Hank was a friend, Karen was not. Georgia meant it as a compliment, meant to say that passion was always superior. But Karen saw instead the simple fact she had been avoiding: Georgia was not a friend. And if she had learned one miserable thing by her age, it was that sexual passion was the least enduring passion of all. Sometimes a lifetime of love was built on top of it — she flashed on the image of Helen at Lara's gravesite, pressing the bunch of irises to her chest — but sometimes it was all there was. And yet, so many people — otherwise reasonable, intelligent people — still made sexual heat the measure of love. Karen had done it herself with Georgia. How stupid, really, when sex was just a jumble of chemicals and some sweat. Lust did not earn you what only years of simple attentiveness and kindness — the harder, humbler stuff — did. She felt clammy all over, and shivered. "Chris's best friend died unexpectedly two weeks ago," she said, realizing that Georgia would have no idea why she was interjecting this now. She wasn't sure herself, except that it had taken over all their thoughts, was forcing them to all see their lives anew.

"Oh, Lord, I'm so sorry," Georgia said, reaching quickly across the table to take Karen's hand.

Karen eased her hand free, and tried to rub away a headache gathering over her eyes.

"Look, I understand. Of course you want to be with her now. And maybe for good," Georgia whispered. Karen heard the note of pleading in her voice. "But — and I know you know this — sometimes the things we plan for so carefully are all wrong for us, and the things that seem the most disruptive . . . well, that's what I fought against for so long." Georgia reached down and turned over to Karen a small, flat package, wrapped in brown paper. "I want you to have this, however things turn out."

"What is it?"

"Why don't you open it?"

Karen took the package and knew from the feel of it that it was a painting. She tore it open carefully. It was the hummingbird, the one she had admired when she first stepped into Georgia's gallery. It made her head spin. She knew how much Georgia loved it. "Oh, I can't—"

"You can, and you must. I want you to have it."

Karen stared down at the painting. It was happening just the way she feared. Everyone got hurt, no one was happy. "Chris needs me now," was all she could say. But what she didn't say was what she was realizing she felt most strongly: that she needed Chris now, too.

51

*H*elen dimly recognized the man standing on her doorstep, but she couldn't place him, and she couldn't work up the effort to try. Emma greeted him like an old friend, though, swaying her backside extravagantly, so Helen took her cue and managed a smile. "I'm sorry, I know we've met," she said, shielding her eyes with her hand as she squinted out at the too-bright day. The hot breath of the afternoon hovered at the threshold.

"Mac, ma'am," he said. He wore a pink and tan plaid shirt and his fists bulged in the pockets of his pressed khaki shorts. "Hey, girl," he said, squatting to let Emma lick his face while he patted her vigorously on the rump. From her vantage, Helen could see his freckled scalp, with what was left of his hair combed in wispy white strands across the span of it. He had probably been a handsome man once, she guessed, but age, hard work, and unhappiness had made him loose-jowled and gaunt. "Remember, I came and fixed your window one day?" he said, standing up again. "And you gave me a piece of your terrific pie."

She could conjure only a dim flicker, but it registered as searing pain, anyway. Any reminder of the life she used to have, when Lara was still alive, shreded her up that way.

"Maybe this is a bad time . . . Helen. But I, uh . . . I wanted to come pay my respects, say how sorry I am for your loss."

She watched him swallowing hard, clenching his jaw. Then she remembered: he was the widower. She had told Lara about him, about how he'd cried while talking about his dead wife. It had moved her then, and scared her, but she had been able to reassure herself: this is not yet my dark burden. Not yet.

"Come in, Mac," Helen said. "I've just mixed a pitcher of iced tea."

"If it's no trouble," he said. She settled him in the living room with Emma, who calmly laid across his feet, and headed into the kitchen to make up a tray. Fortunately, it was one of her good days, meaning that she had showered and put on fresh clothes. Since the funeral, all of them — the guys, Chris, Karen, Angie, Ruth, Felicia — had been showing up daily, armed like the Red Cross with sweet soaps and snacks, thinking, Helen supposed, that she'd be prompted by the visits to make herself presentable, to find meaning again in ordinary daily rituals. But what did they know? None of them had crossed over to her side. She didn't give a thought to what they made of her derelict state, and if she did at all, it was only to hope that maybe it would repel them enough to stay away. But ever since the garage incident, the whole gang had collectively put their foot down, and Ruth got her a prescription for an antidepressant. She took it only occasionally, though, since it unnerved her to think of genuine emotion — even when it was unbearable — as nothing but a chemical reaction that could be manipulated by a pill.

It wasn't that she disliked all her friends suddenly, but seeing them accomplished only two things, both terrible: it reminded her that she was now some freakish amputee, while they were still paired, whole; and it deprived her of the solitude she needed to hoard and hone her memories of Lara. Every day, the only preserve of pleasure left to her was to rewind and relive their life together in her head. She was portioning it out, starting chronologically, letting herself savor again their meeting, their first years of living together, their trips, even the disappointments and the arguments. Some days the images were so vivid, she just lay there, with Emma across the foot of the bed, drifting in and out of waking dreams and sleeping dreams, the memories continuous. That made the gang's visits irrelevant, and the functions they urged on her — eating, drinking, bathing — all so pointless. Without Lara, there was no reason to go on. It was not a tragedy, it was simple fact. And Felicia had meddled most unforgivably, because Helen knew she had courage only once to design and summon her own death. Now that she'd been "saved," she'd have to wait like everyone else, be patient for death's own timing.

"Here we are," Helen said, putting the tray down

on the coffee table in front of Mac. She sat across from him in one of the swivel club chairs, struggling, for his sake, to shake her somber mood.

Mac raised his glass and drained half of it in one long, noiseless gulp. Then he put it down and began gently punching his fist into his palm. "You know, I was a farmer all my life," he said. "My business was bringing things to life, and keeping them alive." He looked up at her shyly. "I didn't used to think of it that way. I used to think of it as purely production and profit. And then Dorothy died."

Emma, sensitive to inflection, Helen knew, sat up and rested her head on Mac's knee. Mac stroked her head absently.

"In the beginning, I didn't know how to live my old life without Dorothy," Mac said. "And I sure didn't have a new one, either. A lot of people say they know what you're going through. But they don't. I do, though. I've got a passport stamped from where you are. I believe I can help you."

Helen felt a small twist of hope, some part of which was made of the fanciful notion that he knew how to bring Lara back. The comedown from those moments — because she'd had dreams from which she woke with the joyful illusion that Lara was still alive — was too sharply painful. If she had had any say in it, she would never have those mirages again — no matter how dazzling the delusion was of Lara's resurrection — because they made it that much more suffocating to return to the monotonous ache of her daily grief. She was hollowed out, spooned clean, and rebuilt, joint by joint, with sorrow. No other feeling could last inside her; hope and happiness were extinguished on contact. "You're a good man, Mac,"

Helen said. "I have no reason to be rude to you. But no one can help. Nothing matters. Maybe you don't remember that part anymore."

"You made me begin to forget."

Helen crossed her arms tightly. "You're on totally the wrong track, Mac—"

"I'm not suggesting anything like romance," he said, his tone scolding. "I wouldn't mind your friendship, though. But mostly I'm thinking of something practical, a pooling of resources, the way you'd do in nature. You and me—we don't both need two big places. I could take care of whichever one we lived in. I could give Emma her walks till you get your spirit back. I could—I don't know—make bread and listen to you talk."

She had that sensation again that she dreaded—wanting to tell Lara something and then realizing she couldn't—in this case, how extremely odd, and yet touching, Mac's proposition was. "Why wouldn't I move in with one of my old friends if I wanted company?" she asked, as kindly as possible. "After all, you and I are strangers, really."

"Move in with a couple? You know you can't do that. Same as I know it. We weren't made to live in trios. Even, not odd, numbers rule in nature. The urge to pair off is strong down to the tiniest microbe." He rubbed the back of his neck. "I'm sorry if I'm offending you. I worried that you might not be ready to hear this. Maybe I came too soon. But I figured it was better than coming too late." He stood up. Emma jumped to her feet, too, and looked at Helen expectantly.

Helen called Emma over and massaged her ears. "She probably would love one of her long walks. You

219

miss Lara, too, don't you?" she said, dripping a hot
tear onto the top of the dog's silky head. "Take her
out for a little walk, would you, Mac?" After all, Helen
thought, just because she had herself given up on joy,
that didn't mean everyone else around her had to, too.

52

*B*ill Seagirt had never packed a suitcase for himself in his entire married life, and this time was no exception. Bunny had told him last night that she was throwing him out, but he literally didn't know how to go. She was forced to pack up his stuff herself, and by the time she was finished, she had three bulging bags that she dragged, two-fisted, to the front door.

He was still sitting on the living room couch, looking out the sliding glass doors to the pool. He hadn't moved from that spot since last night, when she had told him — at the top of her lungs — that she was divorcing him. He had screamed back that she was being ridiculous, that the fling with Sissy was no different from the scores of others he'd had all throughout their marriage. That was probably, he conceded now, the wrong defense to have launched.

Except that he had meant it. He was just not a man cut out for monogamy. It hadn't hurt their marriage — the fact that Bunny had never known, until Sissy decided to blab, was evidence of that. He had always been there for Bunny in every way she expected a husband to be. He had never missed a nightly meal, let alone a holiday. He had always had enough money and sex drive for two women at once. He had never been indiscreet.

He could have borne it better, perhaps, if he had been found out with Angie, if only he had gotten that far with her. Angie, he imagined, would have been worth it. But to have his marriage dismantled over Sissy Armonk and her torpedo breasts — it was just too hard to accept.

"Bunny, look —"

"Get out," she said, one hand on her hip, the other holding open the front door.

"Bunny, after all these years together —"

"You're a fraud, Bill. A mere husband impersonator. Tell it to my lawyer."

"Bunny —"

"Right now, Bill. You're polluting the air in my house."

"*Your* house! You never worked a day in your life."

"It's mine, now. I bought it with a clause called 'mental cruelty.' To think that while I was going door-to-door trying to uphold the moral fabric of this community, you were running around to the back doors, with your BVDs around your knees —"

"Bunny, it wasn't like that!" He stood, sucked in his

stomach, and strode over to look her in the eye. "Don't you have any feelings left for me?"

"Yes, and they're all violent. Get out before I call the police and have you charged with trespassing." She began shoving and kicking his suitcases out the door.

"You'll regret this, Bunny," he said. "You'll end up a lonely old woman!"

"Thanks to you, I've been a lonely old woman for years, only I didn't know it. Now at least I can do something about it." When she slammed the front door closed, it came within an inch of hitting him in the nose.

53

*A*ngie held out the color brochure in front of Helen, pulling it taut against the light breeze coming in off the bay. "It's completely gay and lesbian owned, run and occupied," Angie said, glancing at Ruth for support. "It's about an hour south of here. The houses are gorgeous, but won't cost us much more than we paid here. And the people are great, from all over the country. There's a clubhouse where the bookshelves and video center are crammed with queer titles. Even the pool towels are lavender."

"There were more same-sex couples walking around hand in hand than we'd ever seen — even in the Village," Ruth chimed in. "Oh, God, Helen — I'm so sorry!"

Angie scowled at Ruth, and quickly turned back to

squeeze Helen's hand. "She just meant you'd — we'd all — be perfectly at home," Angie said. Helen shifted on her beach chair and kept looking out at the water, its surface flecked with coral as the sun began to sink down to meet the horizon. Angie wished Helen would take off her sunglasses, so she could better gauge her reaction.

"I won't be perfectly at home anywhere, anymore," Helen said. "At any rate, it would take more than lavender towels. Lakeside Leisure is the last place Lara was alive. I don't want to leave that."

Angie felt her resolve freeze up. In her lifetime, she'd faced down psycho-bigots, local police and co-op boards but nothing so far had proven as intractable or impenetrable as Helen's grief. Angie heard herself somehow always saying the wrong thing, or at least never thinking of the right thing. She felt acutely the contempt Helen held them all in, and found herself mourning twice: first, the physical loss of Lara, and now, the spiritual loss of Helen, who seemed gone to them in all the ways they'd known and loved.

"Helen," Ruth said, "we want you — very badly — to come with us. We haven't bought any house there yet, because we want you to live with us, share a house with us, if that's what you want. We thought we'd get something bigger, so you can have the privacy of your own suite."

"Of course, you can always get your own place, too, if you like that better, right next door or down the block or something," Angie said, buoyed by Ruth's start. "And we'll do everything we can to help you with the paperwork and the packing and everything. Just please, please, say you'll come with us."

Angie watched as Helen reached down and scooped

up a handful of sand and poured it slowly back. She kept at it for several minutes, as if mesmerized by the motion. "I know you two were the least enthusiastic about retiring here," Helen said. "But you don't have to feel guilty about leaving now that you've found a place you like better. Or now that I've been widowed. I don't want anyone putting her life on hold for me. Besides, I've got other friends here. And I'll come visit, I promise."

"Helen, the guys are thinking of moving with us, too," Angie said gently. She wasn't sure they had told Helen yet, since Rich, especially, was guilt-wracked about it. But he'd admitted he'd gotten superstitious in his old age. He felt he hadn't really deserved to leave New York alive—not with all the friends he'd lost to AIDS who hadn't lived differently from the way he had. Lara's heart attack, he'd said, made him feel death was on his heels again, and his instinct was to flee.

"I know about the guys," Helen said, lifting up her sunglasses and resting them on top of her head. "They've already made me the same offer." She smiled.

Angie folded up the brochure, angrily snapping it at the creases. "Oh, so who are your friends here, then? If you're counting on Chris and Karen, I wouldn't. They're not going to last more than a few more minutes."

"Felicia. Mac. I count them," Helen said. "I'm not *not* counting you guys, but you're leaving. And as far as place goes, one's just the same as another to me, Angie. Happiness is not found in a place."

"Look, Helen, this is about more than just a place, and you know it," Angie said, helpless now to hide her impatience. "These old straight people—they don't know what you're going through. You want them to start fixing you up with the widowers with hair growing out of their ears? Huh?"

Ruth squeezed Angie's knee, a familiar warning signal. "Helen," Ruth said, "I think it would be healthy for you to be in a new setting. My God, every time you look out at your garden alone —"

"I don't want to forget!" Helen said, scrambling to her feet. "That's what this is all about, isn't it? You all want me to just get on with my life. Well, I've lived my life already, and now it's over." She pounded down the beach to the shoreline and headed away from them at a brisk pace.

"Don't go after her," Ruth said, grabbing Angie's arm as she started to rise. "Let her be."

Angie sat back down in her chair reluctantly and watched till Helen was a distant stick figure, indistinguishable from the other beachcombers in the dusk.

54

*F*elicia sat on the couch and accepted the cup of tea Bunny offered. "Thanks for coming over, Felicia, dear," Bunny said. "I know we haven't been on the best of terms lately and well, you know me, I don't like to leave bad feelings hanging in the air between friends."

Felicia glowered. "Bunny, if there are bad feelings hanging around, they are emanating directly from you. Save your speeches for your next hateful petition. What is it that you want from me?"

Bunny leaned back in her club chair and touched her fingertips delicately to her chiffon, floral-print blouse. "I am shocked — *shocked* — by what you're implying."

"I'm not implying a damn thing, Bunny Seagirt. I'm accusing you outright."

"Well! I will not let you drag me into your sour mood, Felicia. I asked you here because I need your advice."

Felicia sipped her tea, perched on the edge of the couch to telegraph her eagerness to leave quickly.

"I don't know if you've heard about my unfortunate circumstances," Bunny said.

"Your divorce? Everyone's heard. Bill is practically giving press conferences at the clubhouse, saying he's leaving you because you're frigid. He said every woman in Florida was willing to spread for him, except his wife — and the dykes." Felicia blushed at repeating Bill's crude language, but it was worth it to see Bunny's mouth fall open and stay that way for an unattractive minute.

"How *dare* he! How dare he speak about me in the same breath with those deviants."

"Oh, Bunny, you never learn, do you?" Felicia stood up.

"No — don't go, Felicia. I'm sorry, I — look, I need your help. Sit back down. Please. Thank you. More tea?"

"No. What is it, already, Bunny?"

"Well," Bunny said, sighing extravagantly, "since it appears you know of my circumstances, you can imagine that I'm in the market for a good divorce lawyer. A dynamite one, actually."

Felicia waited, her hands tightly around her knees, having no idea where Bunny was headed.

"And I've been making some calls and I keep getting recommended to Chris Waters who is, apparently, a friend of your friend Helen's."

"You've got to be kidding, Bunny—"

"I know it looks hypocritical, given my position on their lifestyle, but it could work well for me in two ways. For starters, I can't bear to use anybody in the area who's known us all these years. It's just too humiliating, frankly. Secondly, it seems to me that this Chris Waters person would have an inborn hostility to the man in question here—"

"Bunny, you haven't got as much sense as a hedge. Why in God's name would any of them want to help you?"

"Because I can pay a lot of money. Anything to crucify Bill Seagirt, who has made a mockery of my devotion and the entire institution of marriage!"

"And none of this has made you think for a second that maybe it's people who make a marriage, and not the stupid institution—whatever that is."

"You're wrong. Some people are just unworthy of the institution. My husband, unfortunately, was one of them. But it doesn't make those dykes any more worthy of it, no matter how pathetically they play at housekeeping together."

Felicia felt her cheeks tighten with heat. She fantasized about beating Bunny over the head with the coffee table. "The only pathetic thing here, Bunny, is how you wouldn't recognize the value of love if it bit you in the butt. When my son married a black girl—" Bunny's eyes widened in what was clearly shock and revulsion— "I marveled at the power of love, how

230

helpless and humble we must all be before it. My daddy always preached that, but I never really saw it with my own eyes till I watched my son and his fiancée together. Because I knew what they were both going to have to go through to honor that love. And how brave and right they are to do it. Same as these couples in Paxton Court. And you aren't fit to breathe the air in the same room with them, Bunny Seagirt."

"Felicia! Where is your loyalty to your own kind?"

"My own kind are decent people, Bunny. That's who I feel loyalty to. Not only won't I help you get Chris as your lawyer, but I'm going to do my damndest right now to see if Chris will represent Bill!"

"Felicia, it's scary to me that you've become a homosexual sympathizer!"

"You could be onto something there, Bunny. Why don't you try a little sympathy with your own son?"

"How *dare* you? My son is not a homosexual!"

"Bill's gone on quite a bit about that, too, Bunny. How you turned his son into a flaming faggot, as he puts it."

"Oh, dear Lord," Bunny said, leaning forward to rock her head in her hands. "That man will stop at nothing. The filthy, filthy lies."

"Don't you see, Bunny? If the two of you would just love your son, you wouldn't have to torture each other with blame over something that doesn't warrant blame."

"What would you know about it, Felicia? Although I guess you're nearly as bad off as I am — having half-breed grandchildren. Maybe that's worse than having none at all."

For a good minute, Felicia stood rigid, rage washing over her like scalding water. She was angry at more

231

than Bunny and her stupidity. She was angry at God, for taking Lara away from Helen, and letting someone like Bunny continue to pollute the planet. She refused to be reduced to saying cruel things on top of cruel things. She strode to the door and slammed it shut behind her. Bunny Seagirt was perfectly capable of making her life miserable all by herself.

55

*C*hris walked slowly through the house in the direction of Karen's voice. Karen was calling her, from the vicinity of the sun room. Chris had dimly noticed that Karen had been spending a lot of time painting again, after having put it aside for several weeks. But Chris didn't venture in there at all anymore. She had even stopped herself from wondering what Karen was up to. She half hoped Karen had taken it on herself to be packing quietly, so it would all be accomplished neatly one morning, and half hoped Karen hadn't heard her angry words at all. Either way, Chris hadn't had the stamina to either finish or repair the rift between them. Mourning Lara drained her of all her resources, and time spent with Helen — far from helping either of them heal — just seemed to set them both back. They both wanted whatever particular combination of gestures, ideas, neuroses, humor, and energy it was that made up Lara, and it only disappointed them both when neither was able to somehow conjure her.

Karen was standing at her easel, the sun on her hair, making her look as innocent as a child. Chris suddenly felt such longing that she thought she might sag to the floor at her feet.

"Well, aren't you going to say anything?" Karen asked, grinning timidly.

"About what?" Chris asked, but then answered her own question with a glance. On the easel was a portrait of her. The resemblance was eerily accurate, and Chris was in awe all over again of Karen's talent. But there was something else, too, because the face on the canvas had a kind of noble bearing, a courage and compassion Chris did not see when she looked in the mirror. Yet somehow the brush strokes, the arrangement of light and dark, communicated that. "It's, uh . . ." Chris just shook her head.

"The best thing I've ever done," Karen said, turning to regard it. "It was a labor of love. The only one that ever was."

Chris steeled herself, desperate not to betray any emotion. She moved closer, keeping her eyes on the painting. But Karen seized her hand as soon as she was close enough. "I'm sorry," she said, her voice spongy with tears. "For everything. Can we start over? Please let me stay. Let me" — her voice broke and she covered her face with her free hand — "love you again."

Only a few inches stood between her and Karen, and yet that simple distance, Chris knew, held the power to change the course of the rest of both their lives. The wound was still raw from Lara's death, and the pull of retreat, the lure of fleeing to safety from any risk of pain, was strong. But before Chris had any real chance to debate, some instinct made her cradle Karen's head on her shoulder and circle her with her arms as she cried. There were no guarantees, she knew, but as long as they were both alive, they could try.

56

*T*he moving van was back in Paxton Court, and as Felicia neared, she could see T-shirted men, their shoulders slick with sweat, as they pushed and climbed and scrambled up and down the loading ramp. It was an enormous truck — Felicia imagined it would be as tall as a skyscraper if it were upright — but it needed to be because, as Helen had explained, it was moving both couples — Rudy and Rich and Angie and Ruth — at the same time.

Helen didn't say it, but Felicia knew she could use moral support today as her friends prepared to leave for their new retirement homes. Felicia was sorry to see them go, too. She wished they would give Lakeside Leisure another chance, especially since Bunny Seagirt had decided, once her divorce was final and the house was hers free and clear, to move somewhere else where half the widows wouldn't have seen her ex-husband's private parts.

"No, no, forget it — give it to me to put in the car," Rudy was shouting at one of the moving men who had slung a cloisonne lamp over his shoulder like a sack of flour.

"Rudy, you can't take *everything* in the car. There's not going to be room for us soon," said a shirtless Rich, dabbing at his forehead with a purple tank top he had apparently been, until moments ago, wearing.

Helen was sitting on her front steps, Emma next to her, as Felicia made her way up the walk. The dog lowered her ears in happy greeting. "Is there room there on the bleachers for another spectator?" Felicia asked.

"For you, always," Helen said, scooting over and patting the cement next to her.

"Hey, lady, what's this picture mean?" another of the movers shouted, this time to Angie. He held up, with a bowling-pin shaped forearm, a framed poster with the slogan, "A woman without a man is like a fish without a bicycle."

Angie whirled around from directing two other men who were hauling her black lacquer wall unit. "Oh, that," she said over her shoulder. "It's an environmental protection poster."

"Oh," he said, marching on, apparently satisfied.

"Has it been this way all morning?" Felicia asked.

Helen smiled. "Pretty much. Ruth seems to be hiding out in the house now, though, because Angie kept getting angry when she would start laughing at her explanations to the movers. I told her she should be grateful that at least the books were packed away."

237

They watched a while longer before Felicia spoke again. "You're going to move down to be with them eventually, aren't you?" she asked.

Helen looked startled. "I haven't said a word to anybody about it."

"But it's the right thing to do," Felicia said. "Lara exists in all of your memories together, more than she does here."

Helen's eyes turned glassy with tears. "I didn't want to, at first. Lara and I had this idea that people all ought to be able to live together. It seemed like progress. I didn't want to betray that."

"But you're going to be with friends," Felicia said. "Everybody's entitled to that. And friends have things in common. One way or another."

Helen nodded. "That's why I know you and I'll stay in touch."

"That's right, dear." Felicia missed Helen already, just thinking about it. "When will you go?"

"I figure I'll be ready in a few months. And maybe by then Chris and Karen will feel solid enough again to come, too."

"Paxton Court won't be the same without you, of course," Felicia said.

"That should make a lot of people happy," Helen said.

"Well, not me and Ted. Not Mac. Not Georgia."

"That's not a bad lineup of friends, after all, in such a short time," Helen said.

"It doesn't take long to start caring about people."

"But it takes forever to stop, doesn't it?" Helen said.

Felicia smiled, and slipped an arm around Helen's waist. "Only when you're really, really lucky."

A few of the publications of
THE NAIAD PRESS, INC.
P.O. Box 10543 • Tallahassee, Florida 32302
Phone (904) 539-5965
Toll-Free Order Number: 1-800-533-1973
Mail orders welcome. Please include 15% postage.

PAXTON COURT by Diane Salvatore. 256 pp. Erotic and wickedly funny contemporary tale about the business of learning to live together. ISBN 1-56280-109-0 $21.95

PAYBACK by Celia Cohen. 176 pp. A gripping thriller of romance, revenge and betrayal. ISBN 1-56280-084-1 10.95

THE BEACH AFFAIR by Barbara Johnson. 224 pp. Sizzling summer romance/mystery/intrigue. ISBN 1-56280-090-6 10.95

GETTING THERE by Robbi Sommers. 192 pp. Nobody does it like Robbi! ISBN 1-56280-099-X 10.95

FINAL CUT by Lisa Haddock. 208 pp. 2nd Carmen Ramirez mystery. ISBN 1-56280-088-4 10.95

FLASHPOINT by Katherine V. Forrest. 256 pp. A Lesbian blockbuster! ISBN 1-56280-079-5 10.95

DAUGHTERS OF A CORAL DAWN by Katherine V. Forrest. Audio Book — read by Jane Merrow. ISBN 1-56280-110-4 16.95

CLAIRE OF THE MOON by Nicole Conn. Audio Book —Read by Marianne Hyatt. ISBN 1-56280-113-9 16.95

FOR LOVE AND FOR LIFE: INTIMATE PORTRAITS OF LESBIAN COUPLES by Susan Johnson. 224 pp. ISBN 1-56280-091-4 14.95

DEVOTION by Mindy Kaplan. 192 pp. See the movie — read the book! ISBN 1-56280-093-0 10.95

SOMEONE TO WATCH by Jaye Maiman. 272 pp. A Robin Miller mystery. 4th in a series. ISBN 1-56280-095-7 10.95

GREENER THAN GRASS by Jennifer Fulton. 208 pp. A young woman — a stranger in her bed. ISBN 1-56280-092-2 10.95

TRAVELS WITH DIANA HUNTER by Regine Sands. Erotic lesbian romp. Audio Book (2 cassettes) ISBN 1-56280-107-4 16.95

CABIN FEVER by Carol Schmidt. 256 pp. Sizzling suspense and passion. ISBN 1-56280-089-1 10.95

THERE WILL BE NO GOODBYES by Laura DeHart Young. 192 pp. Romantic love, strength, and friendship. ISBN 1-56280-103-1 10.95

FAULTLINE by Sheila Ortiz Taylor. 144 pp. Joyous comic
lesbian novel.   ISBN 1-56280-108-2   9.95

OPEN HOUSE by Pat Welch. 176 pp. P.I. Helen Black's fourth
case.   ISBN 1-56280-102-3   10.95

ONCE MORE WITH FEELING by Peggy J. Herring. 240 pp.
Lighthearted, loving romantic adventure.   ISBN 1-56280-089-2   10.95

FOREVER by Evelyn Kennedy. 224 pp. Passionate romance — love
overcoming all obstacles.   ISBN 1-56280-094-9   10.95

WHISPERS by Kris Bruyer. 176 pp. Romantic ghost story
                                        ISBN 1-56280-082-5   10.95

NIGHT SONGS by Penny Mickelbury. 224 pp. A Gianna
Maglione Mystery. Second in a series.   ISBN 1-56280-097-3   10.95

GETTING TO THE POINT by Teresa Stores. 256 pp. Classic
southern Lesbian novel.   ISBN 1-56280-100-7   10.95

PAINTED MOON by Karin Kallmaker. 224 pp. Delicious
Kallmaker romance.   ISBN 1-56280-075-2   10.95

THE MYSTERIOUS NAIAD edited by Katherine V. Forrest &
Barbara Grier. 320 pp. Love stories by Naiad Press authors.
                                        ISBN 1-56280-074-4   14.95

DAUGHTERS OF A CORAL DAWN by Katherine V. Forrest.
240 pp. Tenth Anniversay Edition.   ISBN 1-56280-104-X   10.95

BODY GUARD by Claire McNab. 208 pp. A Carol Ashton Mystery.
6th in a series.   ISBN 1-56280-073-6   10.95

CACTUS LOVE by Lee Lynch. 192 pp. Stories by the beloved
storyteller.   ISBN 1-56280-071-X   9.95

SECOND GUESS by Rose Beecham. 216 pp. An Amanda Valentine
Mystery. 2nd in a series.   ISBN 1-56280-069-8   9.95

THE SURE THING by Melissa Hartman. 208 pp. L.A. earthquake
romance.   ISBN 1-56280-078-7   9.95

A RAGE OF MAIDENS by Lauren Wright Douglas. 240 pp. A
Caitlin Reece Mystery. 6th in a series.   ISBN 1-56280-068-X   10.95

TRIPLE EXPOSURE by Jackie Calhoun. 224 pp. Romantic drama
involving many characters.   ISBN 1-56280-067-1   9.95

UP, UP AND AWAY by Catherine Ennis. 192 pp. Delightful
romance.   ISBN 1-56280-065-5   9.95

PERSONAL ADS by Robbi Sommers. 176 pp. Sizzling short
stories.   ISBN 1-56280-059-0   9.95

FLASHPOINT by Katherine V. Forrest. 256 pp. Lesbian
blockbuster!   ISBN 1-56280-043-4   22.95

CROSSWORDS by Penny Sumner. 256 pp. 2nd Victoria Cross
Mystery.   ISBN 1-56280-064-7   9.95

SWEET CHERRY WINE by Carol Schmidt. 224 pp. A novel of
suspense.   ISBN 1-56280-063-9   9.95

CERTAIN SMILES by Dorothy Tell. 160 pp. Erotic short stories.
                                        ISBN 1-56280-066-3   9.95

EDITED OUT by Lisa Haddock. 224 pp. 1st Carmen Ramirez
Mystery.   ISBN 1-56280-077-9   9.95

WEDNESDAY NIGHTS by Camarin Grae. 288 pp. Sexy
adventure.   ISBN 1-56280-060-4   10.95

SMOKEY O by Celia Cohen. 176 pp. Relationships on the
playing field.   ISBN 1-56280-057-4   9.95

KATHLEEN O'DONALD by Penny Hayes. 256 pp. Rose and
Kathleen find each other and employment in 1909 NYC.
                                        ISBN 1-56280-070-1   9.95

STAYING HOME by Elisabeth Nonas. 256 pp. Molly and Alix
want a baby . . . or do they?   ISBN 1-56280-076-0   10.95

TRUE LOVE by Jennifer Fulton. 240 pp. Six lesbians searching
for love in all the "right" places.   ISBN 1-56280-035-3   10.95

GARDENIAS WHERE THERE ARE NONE by Molleen Zanger.
176 pp. Why is Melanie inextricably drawn to the old house?
                                        ISBN 1-56280-056-6   9.95

KEEPING SECRETS by Penny Mickelbury. 208 pp. A Gianna
Maglione Mystery. First in a series.   ISBN 1-56280-052-3   9.95

THE ROMANTIC NAIAD edited by Katherine V. Forrest &
Barbara Grier. 336 pp. Love stories by Naiad Press authors.
                                        ISBN 1-56280-054-X   14.95

UNDER MY SKIN by Jaye Maiman. 336 pp. A Robin Miller
mystery. 3rd in a series.   ISBN 1-56280-049-3.   10.95

STAY TOONED by Rhonda Dicksion. 144 pp. Cartoons — 1st
collection since Lesbian Survival Manual.   ISBN 1-56280-045-0   9.95

CAR POOL by Karin Kallmaker. 272pp. Lesbians on wheels
and then some!   ISBN 1-56280-048-5   10.95

NOT TELLING MOTHER: STORIES FROM A LIFE by Diane
Salvatore. 176 pp. Her 3rd novel.   ISBN 1-56280-044-2   9.95

GOBLIN MARKET by Lauren Wright Douglas. 240pp. A Caitlin
Reece Mystery. 5th in a series.   ISBN 1-56280-047-7   10.95

LONG GOODBYES by Nikki Baker. 256 pp. A Virginia Kelly
mystery. 3rd in a series.   ISBN 1-56280-042-6   9.95

FRIENDS AND LOVERS by Jackie Calhoun. 224 pp. Mid-western
Lesbian lives and loves.   ISBN 1-56280-041-8   10.95

THE CAT CAME BACK by Hilary Mullins. 208 pp. Highly
praised Lesbian novel.   ISBN 1-56280-040-X   9.95

BEHIND CLOSED DOORS by Robbi Sommers. 192 pp. Hot,
erotic short stories.   ISBN 1-56280-039-6   9.95

CLAIRE OF THE MOON by Nicole Conn. 192 pp. See the
movie — read the book!   ISBN 1-56280-038-8   10.95

SILENT HEART by Claire McNab. 192 pp. Exotic Lesbian
romance.   ISBN 1-56280-036-1   10.95

HAPPY ENDINGS by Kate Brandt. 272 pp. Intimate conversations
with Lesbian authors.   ISBN 1-56280-050-7   10.95

THE SPY IN QUESTION by Amanda Kyle Williams. 256 pp.
4th Madison McGuire.   ISBN 1-56280-037-X   9.95

SAVING GRACE by Jennifer Fulton. 240 pp. Adventure and
romantic entanglement.   ISBN 1-56280-051-5   9.95

THE YEAR SEVEN by Molleen Zanger. 208 pp. Women surviving
in a new world.   ISBN 1-56280-034-5   9.95

CURIOUS WINE by Katherine V. Forrest. 176 pp. Tenth Anniversary Edition. The most popular contemporary Lesbian love story.
                                               ISBN 1-56280-053-1   10.95
        Audio Book (2 cassettes)   ISBN 1-56280-105-8   16.95

CHAUTAUQUA by Catherine Ennis. 192 pp. Exciting, romantic
adventure.   ISBN 1-56280-032-9   9.95

A PROPER BURIAL by Pat Welch. 192 pp. A Helen Black
mystery. 3rd in a series.   ISBN 1-56280-033-7   9.95

SILVERLAKE HEAT: A Novel of Suspense by Carol Schmidt.
240 pp. Rhonda is as hot as Laney's dreams.   ISBN 1-56280-031-0   9.95

LOVE, ZENA BETH by Diane Salvatore. 224 pp. The most talked
about lesbian novel of the nineties!   ISBN 1-56280-030-2   10.95

A DOORYARD FULL OF FLOWERS by Isabel Miller. 160 pp.
Stories incl. 2 sequels to *Patience and Sarah.* ISBN 1-56280-029-9   9.95

MURDER BY TRADITION by Katherine V. Forrest. 288 pp. A
Kate Delafield Mystery. 4th in a series.   ISBN 1-56280-002-7   10.95

THE EROTIC NAIAD edited by Katherine V. Forrest & Barbara
Grier. 224 pp. Love stories by Naiad Press authors.
                                               ISBN 1-56280-026-4   13.95

DEAD CERTAIN by Claire McNab. 224 pp. A Carol Ashton
mystery. 5th in a series.   ISBN 1-56280-027-2   9.95

CRAZY FOR LOVING by Jaye Maiman. 320 pp. A Robin Miller
mystery. 2nd in a series.   ISBN 1-56280-025-6   9.95

STONEHURST by Barbara Johnson. 176 pp. Passionate regency
romance.   ISBN 1-56280-024-8   10.95

INTRODUCING AMANDA VALENTINE by Rose Beecham.
256 pp. An Amanda Valentine Mystery. First in a series.
                                               ISBN 1-56280-021-3   9.95

UNCERTAIN COMPANIONS by Robbi Sommers. 204 pp.
Steamy, erotic novel.   ISBN 1-56280-017-5   9.95

A TIGER'S HEART by Lauren W. Douglas. 240 pp. A Caitlin
Reece mystery. 4th in a series.   ISBN 1-56280-018-3   9.95

PAPERBACK ROMANCE by Karin Kallmaker. 256 pp. A
delicious romance.   ISBN 1-56280-019-1   9.95

MORTON RIVER VALLEY by Lee Lynch. 304 pp. Lee Lynch
at her best!   ISBN 1-56280-016-7   9.95

THE LAVENDER HOUSE MURDER by Nikki Baker. 224 pp.
A Virginia Kelly Mystery. 2nd in a series.   ISBN 1-56280-012-4   9.95

PASSION BAY by Jennifer Fulton. 224 pp. Passionate romance,
virgin beaches, tropical skies.   ISBN 1-56280-028-0   10.95

STICKS AND STONES by Jackie Calhoun. 208 pp. Contemporary
lesbian lives and loves.   ISBN 1-56280-020-5   9.95
Audio Book (2 cassettes)   ISBN 1-56280-106-6   16.95

DELIA IRONFOOT by Jeane Harris. 192 pp. Adventure for Delia
and Beth in the Utah mountains.   ISBN 1-56280-014-0   9.95

UNDER THE SOUTHERN CROSS by Claire McNab. 192 pp.
Romantic nights Down Under.   ISBN 1-56280-011-6   9.95

GRASSY FLATS by Penny Hayes. 256 pp. Lesbian romance in
the '30s.   ISBN 1-56280-010-8   9.95

A SINGULAR SPY by Amanda K. Williams. 192 pp. 3rd
Madison McGuire.   ISBN 1-56280-008-6   8.95

THE END OF APRIL by Penny Sumner. 240 pp. A Victoria
Cross mystery. First in a series.   ISBN 1-56280-007-8   8.95

HOUSTON TOWN by Deborah Powell. 208 pp. A Hollis
Carpenter mystery.   ISBN 1-56280-006-X   8.95

KISS AND TELL by Robbi Sommers. 192 pp. Scorching stories
by the author of *Pleasures*.   ISBN 1-56280-005-1   10.95

STILL WATERS by Pat Welch. 208 pp. A Helen Black mystery.
2nd in a series.   ISBN 0-941483-97-5   9.95

TO LOVE AGAIN by Evelyn Kennedy. 208 pp. Wildly romantic
love story.   ISBN 0-941483-85-1   9.95

IN THE GAME by Nikki Baker. 192 pp. A Virginia Kelly
mystery. First in a series.   ISBN 1-56280-004-3   9.95

AVALON by Mary Jane Jones. 256 pp. A Lesbian Arthurian
romance.   ISBN 0-941483-96-7   9.95

STRANDED by Camarin Grae. 320 pp. Entertaining, riveting
adventure.   ISBN 0-941483-99-1   9.95

THE DAUGHTERS OF ARTEMIS by Lauren Wright Douglas.
240 pp. A Caitlin Reece mystery. 3rd in a series.
                                         ISBN 0-941483-95-9   9.95

CLEARWATER by Catherine Ennis. 176 pp. Romantic secrets
of a small Louisiana town. ISBN 0-941483-65-7   8.95

THE HALLELUJAH MURDERS by Dorothy Tell. 176 pp. A
Poppy Dillworth mystery. 2nd in a series. ISBN 0-941483-88-6   8.95

SECOND CHANCE by Jackie Calhoun. 256 pp. Contemporary
Lesbian lives and loves. ISBN 0-941483-93-2   9.95

BENEDICTION by Diane Salvatore. 272 pp. Striking, contemporary romantic novel. ISBN 0-941483-90-8   9.95

BLACK IRIS by Jeane Harris. 192 pp. Caroline's hidden past . . .
ISBN 0-941483-68-1   8.95

TOUCHWOOD by Karin Kallmaker. 240 pp. Loving, May/
December romance. ISBN 0-941483-76-2   9.95

COP OUT by Claire McNab. 208 pp. A Carol Ashton mystery.
4th in a series. ISBN 0-941483-84-3   9.95

THE BEVERLY MALIBU by Katherine V. Forrest. 288 pp. A
Kate Delafield Mystery. 3rd in a series. ISBN 0-941483-48-7   10.95

THAT OLD STUDEBAKER by Lee Lynch. 272 pp. Andy's affair
with Regina and her attachment to her beloved car.
ISBN 0-941483-82-7   9.95

PASSION'S LEGACY by Lori Paige. 224 pp. Sarah is swept into
the arms of Augusta Pym in this delightful historical romance.
ISBN 0-941483-81-9   8.95

THE PROVIDENCE FILE by Amanda Kyle Williams. 256 pp.
Second Madison McGuire ISBN 0-941483-92-4   8.95

I LEFT MY HEART by Jaye Maiman. 320 pp. A Robin Miller
Mystery. First in a series. ISBN 0-941483-72-X   10.95

THE PRICE OF SALT by Patricia Highsmith (writing as Claire
Morgan). 288 pp. Classic lesbian novel, first issued in 1952 . . .
acknowledged by its author under her own, very famous, name.
ISBN 1-56280-003-5   9.95

SIDE BY SIDE by Isabel Miller. 256 pp. From beloved author of
Patience and Sarah. ISBN 0-941483-77-0   9.95

STAYING POWER: LONG TERM LESBIAN COUPLES by
Susan E. Johnson. 352 pp. Joys of coupledom. ISBN 0-941-483-75-4   14.95

SLICK by Camarin Grae. 304 pp. Exotic, erotic adventure.
ISBN 0-941483-74-6   9.95

NINTH LIFE by Lauren Wright Douglas. 256 pp. A Caitlin Reece
mystery. 2nd in a series. ISBN 0-941483-50-9   8.95

PLAYERS by Robbi Sommers. 192 pp. Sizzling, erotic novel.
ISBN 0-941483-73-8   9.95

MURDER AT RED ROOK RANCH by Dorothy Tell. 224 pp.
A Poppy Dillworth mystery. 1st in a series. ISBN 0-941483-80-0   8.95

LESBIAN SURVIVAL MANUAL, by Rhonda Dicksion. 112 pp.
Cartoons! ISBN 0-941483-71-1 8.95

A ROOM FULL OF WOMEN by Elisabeth Nonas. 256 pp.
Contemporary Lesbian lives. ISBN 0-941483-69-X 9.95

THEME FOR DIVERSE INSTRUMENTS by Jane Rule. 208 pp.
Powerful romantic lesbian stories. ISBN 0-941483-63-0 8.95

CLUB 12 by Amanda Kyle Williams. 288 pp. Espionage thriller
featuring a lesbian agent! ISBN 0-941483-64-9 8.95

DEATH DOWN UNDER by Claire McNab. 240 pp. A Carol
Ashton mystery. 3rd in a series. ISBN 0-941483-39-8 9.95

MONTANA FEATHERS by Penny Hayes. 256 pp. Vivian and
Elizabeth find love in frontier Montana. ISBN 0-941483-61-4 8.95

LIFESTYLES by Jackie Calhoun. 224 pp. Contemporary Lesbian
lives and loves. ISBN 0-941483-57-6 9.95

WILDERNESS TREK by Dorothy Tell. 192 pp. Six women on
vacation learning ''new'' skills. ISBN 0-941483-60-6 8.95

MURDER BY THE BOOK by Pat Welch. 256 pp. A Helen Black
Mystery. First in a series. ISBN 0-941483-59-2 9.95

THERE'S SOMETHING I'VE BEEN MEANING TO TELL YOU
Ed. by Loralee MacPike. 288 pp. Gay men and lesbians coming out
to their children. ISBN 0-941483-44-4 9.95

LIFTING BELLY by Gertrude Stein. Ed. by Rebecca Mark. 104 pp.
Erotic poetry. ISBN 0-941483-51-7 10.95

AFTER THE FIRE by Jane Rule. 256 pp. Warm, human novel by
this incomparable author. ISBN 0-941483-45-2 8.95

THREE WOMEN by March Hastings. 232 pp. Golden oldie. A
triangle among wealthy sophisticates. ISBN 0-941483-43-6 8.95

PLEASURES by Robbi Sommers. 204 pp. Unprecedented
eroticism. ISBN 0-941483-49-5 8.95

EDGEWISE by Camarin Grae. 372 pp. Spellbinding
adventure. ISBN 0-941483-19-3 9.95

FATAL REUNION by Claire McNab. 224 pp. A Carol Ashton
mystery. 2nd in a series. ISBN 0-941483-40-1 10.95

IN EVERY PORT by Karin Kallmaker. 228 pp. Jessica's sexy,
adventuresome travels. ISBN 0-941483-37-7 9.95

OF LOVE AND GLORY by Evelyn Kennedy. 192 pp. Exciting
WWII romance. ISBN 0-941483-32-0 10.95

CLICKING STONES by Nancy Tyler Glenn. 288 pp. Love
transcending time. ISBN 0-941483-31-2 9.95

SOUTH OF THE LINE by Catherine Ennis. 216 pp. Civil War
adventure. ISBN 0-941483-29-0 8.95

WOMAN PLUS WOMAN by Dolores Klaich. 300 pp. Supurb
Lesbian overview.   ISBN 0-941483-28-2   9.95

THE FINER GRAIN by Denise Ohio. 216 pp. Brilliant young
college lesbian novel.   ISBN 0-941483-11-8   8.95

OCTOBER OBSESSION by Meredith More. Josie's rich, secret
Lesbian life.   ISBN 0-941483-18-5   8.95

BEFORE STONEWALL: THE MAKING OF A GAY AND
LESBIAN COMMUNITY by Andrea Weiss & Greta Schiller.
96 pp., 25 illus.   ISBN 0-941483-20-7   7.95

OSTEN'S BAY by Zenobia N. Vole. 204 pp. Sizzling adventure
romance set on Bonaire.   ISBN 0-941483-15-0   8.95

LESSONS IN MURDER by Claire McNab. 216 pp. A Carol
Ashton mystery. First in a series.   ISBN 0-941483-14-2   9.95

YELLOWTHROAT by Penny Hayes. 240 pp. Margarita, bandit,
kidnaps Julia.   ISBN 0-941483-10-X   8.95

SAPPHISTRY: THE BOOK OF LESBIAN SEXUALITY by
Pat Califia. 3d edition, revised. 208 pp.   ISBN 0-941483-24-X   10.95

CHERISHED LOVE by Evelyn Kennedy. 192 pp. Erotic Lesbian
love story.   ISBN 0-941483-08-8   10.95

THE SECRET IN THE BIRD by Camarin Grae. 312 pp. Striking,
psychological suspense novel.   ISBN 0-941483-05-3   8.95

TO THE LIGHTNING by Catherine Ennis. 208 pp. Romantic
Lesbian 'Robinson Crusoe' adventure.   ISBN 0-941483-06-1   8.95

DREAMS AND SWORDS by Katherine V. Forrest. 192 pp.
Romantic, erotic, imaginative stories. ISBN 0-941483-03-7   8.95

MEMORY BOARD by Jane Rule. 336 pp. Memorable novel
about an aging Lesbian couple.   ISBN 0-941483-02-9   10.95

THE ALWAYS ANONYMOUS BEAST by Lauren Wright Douglas.
224 pp. A Caitlin Reece mystery. First in a series.
                                        ISBN 0-941483-04-5   8.95

THE BLACK AND WHITE OF IT by Ann Allen Shockley.
144 pp. Short stories.   ISBN 0-930044-96-7   7.95

SAY JESUS AND COME TO ME by Ann Allen Shockley. 288
pp. Contemporary romance.   ISBN 0-930044-98-3   8.95

MURDER AT THE NIGHTWOOD BAR by Katherine V. Forrest.
240 pp. A Kate Delafield mystery. Second in a series.
                                        ISBN 0-930044-92-4   10.95

WINGED DANCER by Camarin Grae. 228 pp. Erotic Lesbian
adventure story.   ISBN 0-930044-88-6   8.95

PAZ by Camarin Grae. 336 pp. Romantic Lesbian adventurer
with the power to change the world.   ISBN 0-930044-89-4   8.95

SOUL SNATCHER by Camarin Grae. 224 pp. A puzzle, an
adventure, a mystery — Lesbian romance.   ISBN 0-930044-90-8   8.95

THE LOVE OF GOOD WOMEN by Isabel Miller. 224 pp.
Long-awaited new novel by the author of the beloved *Patience
and Sarah.*   ISBN 0-930044-81-9   8.95

THE HOUSE AT PELHAM FALLS by Brenda Weathers. 240
pp. Suspenseful Lesbian ghost story.   ISBN 0-930044-79-7   7.95

HOME IN YOUR HANDS by Lee Lynch. 240 pp. More stories
from the author of *Old Dyke Tales.*   ISBN 0-930044-80-0   7.95

PEMBROKE PARK by Michelle Martin. 256 pp. Derring-do
and daring romance in Regency England.   ISBN 0-930044-77-0   7.95

THE LONG TRAIL by Penny Hayes. 248 pp. Vivid adventures
of two women in love in the old west.   ISBN 0-930044-76-2   8.95

AN EMERGENCE OF GREEN by Katherine V. Forrest. 288
pp. Powerful novel of sexual discovery.   ISBN 0-930044-69-X   10.95

THE LESBIAN PERIODICALS INDEX edited by Claire Potter.
432 pp. Author & subject index.   ISBN 0-930044-74-6   12.95

DESERT OF THE HEART by Jane Rule. 224 pp. A classic;
basis for the movie *Desert Hearts.*   ISBN 0-930044-73-8   10.95

TORCHLIGHT TO VALHALLA by Gale Wilhelm. 128 pp.
Classic novel by a great Lesbian writer.   ISBN 0-930044-68-1   7.95

LESBIAN NUNS: BREAKING SILENCE edited by Rosemary
Curb and Nancy Manahan. 432 pp. Unprecedented autobiographies
of religious life.   ISBN 0-930044-62-2   9.95

THE SWASHBUCKLER by Lee Lynch. 288 pp. Colorful novel
set in Greenwich Village in the sixties.   ISBN 0-930044-66-5   8.95

SEX VARIANT WOMEN IN LITERATURE by Jeannette
Howard Foster. 448 pp. Literary history.   ISBN 0-930044-65-7   8.95

A HOT-EYED MODERATE by Jane Rule. 252 pp. Hard-hitting
essays on gay life; writing; art.   ISBN 0-930044-57-6   7.95

AMATEUR CITY by Katherine V. Forrest. 224 pp. A Kate
Delafield mystery. First in a series.   ISBN 0-930044-55-X   10.95

THE SOPHIE HOROWITZ STORY by Sarah Schulman. 176 pp.
Engaging novel of madcap intrigue.   ISBN 0-930044-54-1   7.95

THE YOUNG IN ONE ANOTHER'S ARMS by Jane Rule.
224 pp. Classic Jane Rule.   ISBN 0-930044-53-3   9.95

OLD DYKE TALES by Lee Lynch. 224 pp. Extraordinary stories
of our diverse Lesbian lives.   ISBN 0-930044-51-7   8.95

AGAINST THE SEASON by Jane Rule. 224 pp. Luminous,
complex novel of interrelationships.   ISBN 0-930044-48-7   8.95

LOVERS IN THE PRESENT AFTERNOON by Kathleen Fleming.
288 pp. A novel about recovery and growth.   ISBN 0-930044-46-0   8.95

TOOTHPICK HOUSE by Lee Lynch. 264 pp. Love between two
Lesbians of different classes.   ISBN 0-930044-45-2   7.95

CONTRACT WITH THE WORLD by Jane Rule. 340 pp. Power-
ful, panoramic novel of gay life.   ISBN 0-930044-28-2   9.95

THIS IS NOT FOR YOU by Jane Rule. 284 pp. A letter to a
beloved is also an intricate novel.   ISBN 0-930044-25-8   8.95

OUTLANDER by Jane Rule. 207 pp. Short stories and essays by
one of our finest writers.   ISBN 0-930044-17-7   8.95

ODD GIRL OUT by Ann Bannon.   ISBN 0-930044-83-5   5.95
I AM A WOMAN 84-3; WOMEN IN THE SHADOWS 85-1;   each
JOURNEY TO A WOMAN 86-X; BEEBO BRINKER 87-8. Golden
oldies about life in Greenwich Village.

JOURNEY TO FULFILLMENT, A WORLD WITHOUT MEN, and   3.95
RETURN TO LESBOS. All by Valerie Taylor   each

These are just a few of the many Naiad Press titles — we are the oldest and
largest lesbian/feminist publishing company in the world. Please request a
complete catalog. We offer personal service; we encourage and welcome
direct mail orders from individuals who have limited access to bookstores
carrying our publications.